# Risking Exposure

## By Jeanne Moran

*For my sister Joyce, who taught lessons of love, joy, and human dignity without ever saying a word.*

First they came for the Communists
and I didn't speak up because I wasn't a Communist.
Then they came for the trade unionists
and I didn't speak up because I wasn't a trade unionist.
Then they came for the Jews
and I didn't speak up because I wasn't a Jew.
Then they came for me.
By that time, no one was left to speak up.

-Pastor Martin Niemöller

# Chapter One
# Snapshots

## Munich, Germany
## 16 April 1938, Saturday

When Werner ordered me to grab my camera and follow him into the woods, I obeyed. He was the Scharführer, the Master Sergeant. What else could I do?

My best friend Rennie bolted to her feet alongside me. "You don't need to go everywhere Sophie does, Renate," Werner said to her in his usual high-pitched whine. But she ignored him and winked at me as we crashed through the underbrush. Rennie got away with a certain level of disobedience. Younger sisters can.

But I wasn't Werner's sister. I couldn't risk it.

The three of us scared up rabbits and birds as we tromped along. We stopped at a small shed, and there in a hollow lay a large dog the color of a golden sunrise. Several clumps of fur wriggled against her belly.

"Puppies!" Rennie rushed over, dark curls bobbing, squatting so close that the mother lifted her head and growled. Rennie stood and stepped back, her smile undimmed.

Werner crossed his arms as if warding off disease. "The mother doesn't have a tag. Probably a stray."

I watched the tiny pups. Two were still, probably sleeping, one of them pale like its mother. Three others squirmed and nursed, their eyes still closed, their coats dappled in shades of brown and black. "How old do you think they are?" I asked.

Werner didn't answer, just pointed at the ground a short distance from the mother's muzzle. "Photograph that, Adler."

A dark pup, its limp body camouflaged by dirt and decaying leaves. Rennie squatted beside it. "Poor little thing."

I hurried my eyes away from the pitiful creature. "You want a photograph of a dead puppy?" I asked.

"It's an example of nature's way. The mother rejected that pup because he's deformed," he said, his tone matter-of-fact. "He'd do nothing but waste the milk meant for the able-bodied. A useless eater."

A breathy objection came from Rennie. "That's so cruel," she whispered.

But I didn't say anything. I just pulled out Papa's camera and began to adjust my settings. I'd have to look at the poor thing through the camera lens. It might make me sick to my stomach.

Then Rennie's voice brightened. "I think the pup's alive," she said. I lowered my camera.

She cooed at the creature as she made a small bed of leaves around it. Then she lifted and nestled the pup, leaves and all, at the mother's teat, whispering soothing words the whole time. The tiny pup raised its wobbly head and searched until its mouth found nourishment. That's when I saw the deformity – one of the pup's hind legs was mangled, not bloody but sickeningly crooked. This puppy would never walk. I had to turn away.

Werner stepped back and stared at his sister, disgust clear in his squinted eyes and pursed lips. "You're interfering with the natural order of things. Back to camp. And make sure you wash. Who knows what contamination…" He stalked off, shuddering.

As we followed, I stole a backward glance. The mother was using a forepaw to nudge the deformed pup away from her belly, away from her milk. I hurried to catch up with the others.

Rennie and I wove through clusters of boys working in their dirt-streaked uniforms, past rows of tents and campfires. One tent sat apart from the others. It was turned about-face so its back faced the campfires and its flaps faced the woods. Rennie gestured toward it with her thumb. "Werner's," she mouthed. I giggled.

Sure enough, a flap opened and he stepped out, straightened, and marched to the nearest fire. As usual, he was immaculate, his frame, short and wiry for an eighteen-year-old, neatly tucked into a crisp spotless uniform and gleaming shoes. I glanced down at my own scratched shins, the muddy streaks on my leather shoes and the burrs and twigs stuck to my blue uniform skirt. How did he freshen up so quickly? Did he have a clothesline full of pressed uniforms in that tent? I wanted to ask Rennie so we could share another giggle, but his march took him right past us.

He glanced down his long thin nose to his watch. "It's twenty minutes before meal time," he announced to no one in particular. "Are all the girls' troops here?"

Anna, leader of our girl's Jungmädel troop, rose and threw her shoulders back. In an identical announcement tone, she said, "The other troops and their leaders are late. My troop is the only one here on time." She kept her gaze on Werner, no doubt waiting for a compliment about her efficiency. When a few heartbeats passed and the compliment didn't come, she deflated onto a fireside rock.

Rennie whispered, "Anna should forget about nursing school and take up acting."

"But not for an audience of children," I added. In a few days, Anna was leaving her role as Jungmädel leader and none of us girls would be sad to see her go. With us, she'd always been quick with a harsh scolding and slow with a kind word. When adults commented how polite and disciplined we were, she'd smile and soften her voice and tell them how it was all because of her. She alone had sacrificed and slaved to mold us into the fine young girls we were. She alone had taught us to listen and be respectful and responsible. As if our parents hadn't done that from the day we were born.

Rennie agreed. "She puts on a great show for adults."

"Maybe her patients will appreciate her drama," I said. But I doubted it.

Using a thick cake of brown soap, we washed at an old water pump near the campsite. Trudi, one of the youngest girls in our Jungmädel troop, ran up, out of breath. She worked the pump handle to splash the icy water into her filthy cupped hands, then slurped it eagerly.

"What are you doing?" I asked, a little disgusted.

She looked sheepish. "Getting a drink. Lost my canteen."

I didn't want to sound like Anna, so I spoke more gently. "You need to wash with soap and water before you drink from those hands." I pulled my canteen from my rucksack and let her drink all she wanted, then refilled it from the pump. "We can share this," I shook the full canteen, "until we get home."

"You won't tell Anna?"

"It will be our secret," I told Trudi. No sense Trudi getting scolded for an honest mistake. In a few days time, neither of us would ever have to deal with Anna again.

The girls from my troop were scattered among a few different campfires. Trudi joined her little friends where they huddled together, giggling and pointing at the older boys. Rennie gestured toward an adjacent fire and we settled on a couple rocks. That's when I noticed the person stirring the cook pot at our fire was Erich. Erich the Beautiful I called him, but he didn't know that. I felt heat rise to my cheeks and groaned inwardly.

Erich looked up and swept his chocolate eyes between us, smiling. When he spoke, the small cleft in his chin danced. "Food's almost ready."

I was determined to act naturally, not to let on that my pulse was racing. "Smells good. Stew?"

He nodded. "Real campfire stew. Bits of potatoes and carrots, an onion or two, a little meat. Some wild mushrooms collected by that troop," he poked his thumb toward a nearby cluster of boys.

My stepbrother Klaus folded his long frame onto a rock across from me. Rennie chattered to him, sharing details of the exhibit we'd seen earlier that day before we arrived for the cookout. When Rennie took a breath, Klaus turned to me. "You're quiet today, little cat."

Before I could answer, Erich spoke up. "I've always wondered, Klaus," he said as he placidly stirred the stew, "why do you call Sophie 'little cat'?"

One corner of Klaus' mouth lifted and I turned my hot face to the ground. "Sophie used to have this little cat, Minka. When all was quiet, Minka roamed the house, catching mice downstairs in the bakery, sitting in sunbeams in plain sight. But the moment there was trouble, zoom!" he slid one palm forward over the other, "that cat ran and hid and couldn't be found." He smirked. "Sophie's the same way."

Erich stared at the pot, and thankfully the awkwardness ended when Marie and Uta greeted us and perched on nearby stumps. Marie was quite an athlete, keeping her dark hair cropped short in a no-fuss, always-ready-to-run style. If Uta weren't my friend, I'd be jealous of her beauty and confidence. She filled out her white uniform blouse and blue skirt with womanly curves. She smiled flirtatiously as she chatted with the boys at our fire, tossing her nut brown hair and drawing their eyes to the places where its waterfall landed.

We were all fourteen, Uta and Marie and Rennie and me. The three of them had developed, blossomed as my mother would say. Not me. I still had a little girl's contour, pencil straight from top to bottom. I lifted the stubby ends of my straw colored braids, flaring below their elastics like bristles of a paintbrush. I tossed them behind my shoulders.

"So, what will you boys compete in tonight?" Marie flashed her best smile at my stepbrother. She recently started talking about Klaus' defined muscles, the wave of his sandy hair, and the sky blue of his eyes. She was getting as boy crazy as Uta. "Are you boxing, Klaus?"

He nodded and grinned. He'd won a dozen ribbons in Munich boxing competitions. "Boxing and throwing."

"Throwing?"

Klaus peered at her. "We throw rocks for distance and accuracy. It's training for the real thing."

"The real thing," Marie repeated, obviously not understanding.

"Grenades." He grinned at Marie's raised eyebrows. "Does that shock you?"

She nodded. It shocked me as well. I kept forgetting that in another year, Klaus would enter the Wehrmacht, the German Army.

Erich's friendly tone broke the serious mood. "I'm in two races – a wheelbarrow race and a three-legged race."

Klaus sniffed and steadied his gaze on Marie. "Who's more prepared to restore Germany's honor, someone who runs a three-legged race," he glanced at Erich, "or someone who can throw a grenade to a target?"

Erich didn't follow Klaus' lead. "Half the fun of the three-legged race is messing up and falling," he said smiling. "What happens if you mess up with explosives? Pshew!" He blew air past his teeth and threw his hands in the air. Rennie and I giggled, but Marie and Uta didn't. Neither did Klaus.

Three more Jungmädel troops arrived at the campsite and Werner's accusing whine echoed above the chaos. "You're late." He stood atop a rock, hands on hips, overseeing all. "Find a seat so we can eat." The girls and their leaders hurried to obey.

As Scharführer, Werner was the leader of five troops of Hitlerjugend, Hitler Youth boys aged fourteen to eighteen. Even though each girl's troop had its own female leader, he was also in charge of us somehow, all Youth from our Munich neighborhood, boys and girls ages ten to eighteen. That meant he'd still be in charge of us fourteen-year-old girls when we pledged to BDM, Bund Deutscher Mädel, the Hitler Youth branch for girls fourteen to eighteen, in a few days. Once I pledged, I'd be the official Youth photographer for all the troops in our region of Munich. I could hardly wait.

A few of the youngest girls from my troop wandered over looking for a place to eat, including Trudi. I gestured her to sit next to me, then slipped my canteen between us so we could share. She glanced around, looking for Anna no doubt. Once she saw that Anna's attention was fixed on trying to catch Werner's eye, she relaxed. She smiled at me a few times as she sipped from my canteen. We ate our stew in peace.

We were nearly done when the last group of girls finally showed up. Werner's voice cut through the dinnertime chatter. "Falling behind may have cost you girls your dinner. When those who were here on time have finished, you latecomers can eat what's left. If there is anything left." He looked toward our campfire. "You, Lange!"

My stepbrother bolted to his feet, his mess kit clattering to the dirt. "*Ja!*"

"Oversee the clean-up of the meal. Activities begin in," Werner glanced at his watch, "fifteen minutes."

*"Ja, mein Scharführer!"* Klaus strode down the rows of tents, barking orders as mess kits, spoons, and pots clanked and banged.

"You, Adler." Werner pointed at me. "Take photos of tonight's activities for our newsletter."

Quite an honor since I wouldn't take my official position as Youth photographer until I pledged in a few days. I was thrilled, and Rennie squeezed my arm.

Werner's voice whined again, and most of us turned to look at him. "I witnessed a lesson in nature today, a lesson our Fatherland has embraced." He waited until clanking pots and background chatter halted before he continued. "A short time ago, off behind those trees, I found a mother dog and her pups."

Several girls said "Aww." When Werner scowled at them, they quieted and lowered their eyes.

"One of the pups was weak and deformed, a useless eater," he continued. "Its own mother pushed it away so her good milk might be saved for pups which could grow up strong and capable." He stared over his nose, turning slowly to face each cluster of Youth in turn. "Our Fatherland embraces this teaching from the natural world. Germany too is ridding itself of all who would pull strength," he gestured around him, "from strong, capable young like you."

Rennie mumbled something. Abruptly Werner said, "Did you have a something to add, Renate?"

She rose, face flushed. "I brought the deformed pup back to its mother. It was nursing when I left."

I didn't have the heart to tell her what I'd seen.

11

Werner waved a hand dismissively. "Nature will take its course. By now, the mother has probably rid herself of that burden once and for all."

Rennie drew a breath and Erich's brow knit, but they stayed silent. When I rinsed my mess kit a short time later, Erich ducked into the trees.

The activities began on time of course, starting with a parade. We girls sat on the ground and watched as two rows of HJ marched onto the field. I handed Trudi my canteen and faced the oncoming columns of boys with my camera.

Action shots. I wasn't very good at action shots. Adjust settings. Click.

As the Scharführer barked commands, the boys went through maneuvers turning this way and that, performing push-ups and calisthenics, counting their repetitions in unison. I hoped the photos would show activity, not just blurry movement. Adjust settings again. Click.

The boys broke formation and sat with their troops. The competition started with the wheelbarrow race followed by the three-legged race. Click. Click.

Those of us watching cheered and hollered, urging the pairs on, and behind the camera I cheered wildly for Erich. He and his teammate finished second in both races, laughing and clapping each other on the back. Most of the boys in their troop congratulated them, but I noticed Klaus was silent, his lips pressed shut, as if concentrating on something only he could see. A still shot. My favorite. Click.

The next event, the throwing contest, involved one boy from each troop throwing a potato-sized rock. Click. Klaus won by landing his within a meter of the target. I should have been proud but as each rock thudded to earth, I pressed my eyes closed, my mind's lens picturing an explosion.

After some great fun in a baton relay and a piggy back race, two boys from each troop readied for boxing matches. Klaus faced a boy his size, their expressions serious and intimidating. Rennie tugged at my sleeve. "He looks like a regular Max Schmeling."

I grinned at her. "He'd be glad to hear that." Judging by the framed magazine cover on his bedroom wall, Schmeling, a former heavyweight world champion, was Klaus' favorite.

When Werner blew the whistle, all started normally, pairs of boys circling each other, fists at the ready. But within a minute, the five fair contests had turned into brawls with boys shoving each other, staggering, throwing punches as well as kicks. Blood and spittle smeared faces, filth covered uniforms. I watched from my safe place behind the lens, sickened but somehow unable to turn away.

I focused on Klaus. His opponent kicked him square in the shins. Klaus pounced, knocking him onto his back. They grappled and rolled in the dirt, first one of them on top, then the other. In less than a minute, Klaus' opponent was face down and he had sprawled on top, twisting the boy's arm behind him. The boy struggled to free himself, to push up or roll away, but Klaus overpowered him. He yanked the boy's hair, lifting his head to reveal a bloody nose.

Beside me, Rennie made little choking sounds. I knew her thoughts were the same as mine. This wasn't boxing; it wasn't sport. This was a fight.

I used my camera as a spyglass to view the reactions of the other spectators. Most continued to clap and holler their approval, including Marie and Uta and Anna. Little Trudi and her friends sat near the front of the pack, faces hidden behind their hands. Erich watched in stone-faced silence, fists clenched in front of his knees.

Werner stayed focused on the fights, grinning. Finally he blew the whistle and Klaus jumped to his feet and punched his fist in the air. The winner.

It was only then that I realized – I'd watched the whole match hidden behind my camera but hadn't taken any pictures. I might be in trouble for that.

"Last event of the day," Werner announced as the filthy, bloodied fighters staggered and swaggered to rejoin their troops. "The only event in which our guests, the Jungmädel troops, will participate. The human pyramid." He turned to Anna. "Your troop was the first to arrive, so the honored place at the top of the pyramid is yours. To whom does it go?"

Anna rose and straightened. "Renate Müller, *mein Scharführer.*"

I grabbed Rennie's arm as she drew in a breath. Werner's eyebrows shot up. "My sister? Indeed." Then back to business, he gestured to the boys. "One from each troop."

The boys pushed their representative into the open. The three largest boys hunkered on all fours, and two others scrambled on their backs to create the second level.

Werner hooked his finger at Rennie. "Come, Renate."

She rose and slid from my grasp. Everyone bolted to their feet. Voices cheered her on, clamoring for her to hurry up the boys' posed frames to her perch at the top.

She stepped deftly onto one boy's back while reaching to the second row. As she lifted herself and groped for a hand hold, she teetered, off-balance. I held my breath. Several seconds passed and the boys readjusted, steadying the shifting pyramid. One of Rennie's knees reached the back of a boy on the second row. Then she gained purchase and pulled up the other knee to settle on all fours. Once there, she grinned in triumph. A huge cheer rose and I whooshed out my breath.

From the growing shadows behind the pyramid, two pairs of figures appeared, each duo lugging a cook pot. In the blink of an eye, two pots of icy water splashed onto the backsides of those in the pyramid, dousing them, shocking them. The pyramid toppled in a tangle of screams and limbs.

I ran into the wet slippery chaos. "Rennie!" I called. "Rennie, are you all right?"

Relief coursed through me when I found her lying on her back, laughing. She brushed a clump of muddy hair back from her face. "I wondered how I'd get down."

# Chapter Two
# Background

## 20 April, Wednesday

After our BDM pledge ceremony, Rennie and I found my father at the reception behind a table spread with cakes. I leaned into his sideways hug and inhaled. The scents of our family's bakery clung to him, sweetness and yeast breads. Papa's scent.

He kissed my forehead and used my pet name. "Do you feel all right, my Sophiela?"

"I guess that flu's still bothering me." A nagging headache and nuisance body aches had been my companions since the weekend cookout.

He slid pieces of cherry-laden chocolate cake onto plates. "Can you help me serve?"

"Schwarzwälder Kirschtorte! My favorite."

"That's why I made it." He smiled, crinkles around his eyes showing his pleasure. When Werner spotted us and started over, Rennie and I grabbed plates and ducked into the crowd.

"I understand your father is leaving with the Wehrmacht soon," a Party officer said to me.

"Friday," I answered flatly. I didn't want to think about it.

"And he'll be a baker for our glorious soldiers?" another officer asked while chewing my father's confection.

"No, a photographer." A few years earlier, a customer short on cash had taught Papa photography in exchange for some of our bakery's bread. Three lessons later, Papa was hooked. He bought his own camera and sold some shots to local magazines and newspapers. The bakery was our family's livelihood, but photography was Papa's heart.

Mine too, ever since I'd first gone with him to a camera store in Schwabing, Munich's artsy part of town. The shop owner led us into a tiny room in the back and closed the door. He clicked on a lamp which made the room glow orangey red and used tongs to lift a single paper from a liquid-filled tray. As it hung there, dripping, and then was lowered into another tray, something happened. The blank paper filled with faint shadows. The shadows took on shape and substance until there, on that wet paper, was an image I knew from my own mirror – my shy smile and frizzy braids, captured forever by the magic of Papa's camera.

I started squirreling away my delivery tips to buy a camera of my own. In a few weeks, I'd have enough to buy a battered old box camera I'd seen in a pawn shop. Not great quality, but it would be mine.

Rennie and I moved to offer cake to Helga, our troop leader now that we were in BDM. Werner joined us, fisted hands on his hips. "I need Adler to photograph a special HJ event on Monday," he told Helga.

"If it'll help the cause," she said, accepting the cake, her toneless voice obedient but disinterested.

"What's the event?" I asked. I'd have to borrow a camera. Again.

I smelled yeast and felt a gentle nudge behind me. "More cake, anyone?" Papa leaned in, plates in hand. "Last few pieces."

Werner grabbed one without so much as a *danke* and said, "Your daughter's agreed to show the world the wonderful training of our Youth. How discipline and camaraderie make the Reich strong."

Papa turned to me, his steel gray eyes searching my face. He said "Excuse us" to the two leaders, grabbed my elbow, and led me a couple steps away. "Is that what you choose to do, my Sophiela? To help the Scharführer?"

"I'm the Youth photographer now, Papa. The leaders will tell me what events they want photographed." It seemed pretty simple to me.

He dropped his head. "Not you too." Then he lifted his eyes to meet mine and softened his voice almost to a whisper. "You still have a choice. Only you can decide if your choice is worth the cost."

That sounded serious, far too serious with all these people around. I matched his whisper. "I want to practice photography whenever I can."

He nodded thoughtfully. "Then you will need a good camera of your own. Since the Wehrmacht will give me a new one, you may have mine."

I threw my arms around his neck. "Oh, Papa!" His camera was much better quality than that box camera I'd planned to buy. "I'll take good care of it." The two Youth leaders ate their cake with eyebrows raised and heads cocked, pretending not to listen.

"I am not worried about the camera," Papa said, studying my face. "I am worried about..." He hesitated.

"Photograph the truth, my Sophiela. The whole truth. Promise me."

What could be photographed except truth? A camera only sees what's there. I looked Papa in the eyes and promised.

After the reception, everyone in HJ and BDM left for a joint activity. Everyone except me. My parents refused to let me go, saying I'd had enough excitement for one day and needed rest to get over that pesky flu once and for all.

At home in the apartment above our bakery, Mutti closed herself in the bedroom, probably to start her nightly rosary. I set out two china cups and saucers while Papa lit the burner and placed a kettle on the iron stove. He settled a thick black record on the gramophone and lowered the brass tone arm. Noisy scratches gave way to a gentle piano solo. *Für Elise*.

He swept his arms wide and bowed. "May I have this dance, my Sophiela?" I took his hand and right there, in our tiny kitchen, we waltzed.

I closed my eyes. Without my vision, my awareness increased. The high hum of the heating kettle, the delicate music's rhythmic urgings, the yeasty scent on my father's clothing, his hand's steady pressure on my back guiding my dance steps – each expanded and filled me, leaving no room inside for questions about puppies and choices, photos and the whole truth. The questions pushed to my lips and I opened my eyes. "Papa?"

But before I could speak, shouting outside grabbed our attention. A dozen HJ walked down the center of the street, laughing and clapping each other on the back. Klaus was in their midst.

My father bristled. "Go to bed, Sophie." His tight lips and narrowed eyes spelled trouble for Klaus.

Hidden safely in my room, I pressed my ear to the closed door. *Für Elise* scratched to a halt. A clank of metal and a fading whistle meant the kettle was off the stove. A door opened and closed – Klaus was with Papa in the kitchen. "Tell me what you did tonight," Papa demanded.

I could picture Klaus, chin in the air, self-assured. "I was at the Königsplatz on a Youth activity," he said.

"Doing what?"

"What the Scharführer told us to do."

"You smell like smoke. What did you burn?"

Klaus' response was soft. I pressed my ear harder against the door.

"Books!" Papa bellowed. Another door opened and Mutti's voice jumbled with the other two. Papa boomed over the clamor. "Those thugs burned books!" I pictured veins sticking out of Papa's neck, a wild impassioned look on his face. So unlike the everyday Papa who waltzed and drank tea and played the Masters on the Victrola. I wanted to snap a photo of him, of Mutti, of Klaus, of the whole scene.

Klaus spoke up, his voice taunting. "What I do is not your concern, Hans."

I gasped. Calling your stepfather by his first name. Completely disrespectful.

"Go to bed, Klaus. I'll deal with you later." That came from Mutti. Footsteps, then the door next to mine opened and closed. I turned my head and changed ears to listen better. "Why are you giving the boy such a hard time?" my mother demanded. "What Klaus and his troop did, they did in support of our Fatherland and our cause."

"*Our* cause? Yours and mine? The children's?"

"Of course it's our cause. To restore pride to Germany." A lot of adults talked that way, about how the treaty that ended the Great War was unfair and left our country poor and left our people without jobs. They said the Führer and the Party were fixing that, getting rid of job-stealing enemies and restoring our nation's pride.

"Pride? Pride in what? Hoodlums? Bullies who threaten people and destroy property?"

I heard pacing. Papa, no doubt. I didn't need to see my mother to know she'd be standing statuesque with her arms folded and her lips pursed. When Papa spoke again, his voice was softer. "Too bad I must leave so soon. I would rather stay home and guide the children."

Mutti's tone was crisp. "Klaus will serve the Reich by this time next year. He doesn't need guidance. If Sophie does, I'll give it."

"Children need to hear both sides. Then they can decide for themselves."

"What's to decide, Hans? There is only one side. The side for Germany."

"I am on Germany's side." Papa was struggling to keep his voice under control. "Twenty years ago, I fought for the Fatherland in the Great War. I will return to the Wehrmacht in a couple of days."

Mutti sniffed. "Yes, but you won't be fighting. You'll be a photographer." The way she said "photographer" sounded odd to me, as if she mocked it.

21

"The Wehrmacht needs photographers to document the soldiers' lives, Karla, to bring their stories to the newspapers and to the German people."

"Surely they need soldiers more, soldiers who will fight. Why aren't you a soldier?"

I'd wondered that as well. But I never would have asked.

There was a long pause before Papa continued slowly, his voice thick. "Karla, I am a forty-three year old man. I have seen enough fighting. During the war..." He trailed off. "You heard stories, I am sure, from your late husband." He quieted, and when he spoke again his tone held certainty. "I cannot march into another country and use weapons against the people who live there."

This time, it was my mother's voice that boomed. "You're a coward, Hans Adler."

I pressed a hand to my mouth to stifle a gasp. Poor Papa. I wanted to rush to his side, to bury my face in his yeast-scented shirt, to tell him that being my father, a baker, and a photographer was wonderful, that it was enough. But I didn't. I stayed behind my door. Hidden, safe, and silent. Like Minka, my old cat. Shame filled me.

But I didn't move.

Papa cleared his throat. "A true coward never questions what he is told. And cowardice spreads, Karla, like yeast. It grows and expands until it changes the very thing it inhabits..."

I didn't have to wonder what I would have done in Klaus' shoes. With dozens of my friends throwing books onto a bonfire, I would have joined in. Not because of some urge to burn books and get rid of the ideas of our country's enemies. Just to hide in the group by doing what they do. Because refusing to join in would have drawn notice.

Papa would consider me a coward, too. I curled up on my bed and pulled the blankets over my head.

## 21 April, Thursday

The little suspended bell tinkled as I pushed open the bakery door. Mutti was in the food prep area looking quite Mutti-like, her square frame bulging over her calico apron and her hair sculpted into a graying bun. She peeled apples with frightening vigor. "Ah, Sophie. Go set the table." She moved to the front door and flipped the sign to "Closed."

*Eine Kleine Nachtmusik* flowed from our upstairs apartment. I followed its magnetic pull to my father. "Ah, you are home, my Sophiela. How was school?" He gestured me into our apartment with a sweep of his arm, filling me with the aromas of yeast and baked goods. Funny how I didn't notice those same scents downstairs in the bakery. I only noticed them wherever my father was. And he was leaving.

I wanted to talk with him about cowardice and book burning and deformed puppies, but his tone told me I'd need to wait. "You must have heard your mother and me last night," he said, touching my shoulder with such tenderness that I could have wept. "We will talk after dinner." I ducked into the bathroom and splashed water on my face.

After dinner, while I dried my hands, he brought out his camera. "Here, my Sophiela. As promised." Tenderly, he removed the black leather cover and opened the camera's bellows. As he touched each knob and reviewed its purpose and function, he left white smudges on the sharkskin camera body. Flour. Even outside the bakery with his hands clean and his apron off, Papa still got flour on everything. He tugged at the bottom of his shirt and wiped, smearing the tiny grains around.

I placed my hand on his arm. "Please, Papa, don't clean it up. It's perfect." There was so much I wanted to say, so much I wanted to ask. But that darn lump in my throat wouldn't let me.

## 24 April, Sunday

The beautiful spring day was filled with sunshine and promise, the complete opposite of how I felt. Papa had gone to Austria with the Wehrmacht.

After Mass and a midday meal, I stuffed some schoolwork in my jacket pocket and jumped on my bike. My hair hung loose and my jacket unzipped as I rode so both hair and jacket whipped and flapped like wings. Too bad they couldn't lift me and take me away.

I rode for a while through the English Garden Park, past ladies pushing prams and families having picnics. Eventually I found a quiet spot, settled on a bench, and spread the schoolwork across my lap. Math problems would keep me busy until Rennie met me for our weekly bike ride.

Then I noticed – I sat not twenty meters from a familiar scruffy clump of pine trees. How long had it been since I checked the pickle jar for a note from Esther?

I'd taken a few steps toward the trees when I saw him. Klaus strolled down a nearby path toward me. I settled back onto the bench and smoothed the papers into place.

He glanced around at the few nearby people. "Were you sneaking off somewhere, little cat?"

"No," I stammered. I certainly wouldn't tell him about the pickle jar – I had no idea what the consequences might be. "Just stretching my legs. I'm still stiff and achy from that flu. And math gets tedious." I was rambling.

He didn't seem to notice. "Especially tedious on a beautiful Sunday. Do you do homework in the park often?"

"I, I needed a little air. Mutti says fresh air and sunshine clears the head and heals the bones."

He gestured to my tangled hair. "The latest Paris style?" I fumbled for an elastic and pulled my hair into it.

A familiar voice called, "Hi there!" Rennie bicycled to us, waving.

He grinned at her. "My sister is up to something, and she won't tell me what. Please, Renate, talk Sophie out of spending this beautiful Sunday," he emphasized the next few words, "on something useless." With that, he strode away.

Useless. Why did that word bother me so?

Rennie settled in beside me and studied my face. All I could say was, "Something about him…"

"Brothers." She nodded in agreement. "Speaking of brothers, if you promise to keep it a secret, I've got a story about mine." I agreed, of course. "The other day," she began, "Werner scolded the grocer about how the cheeses were arranged." She stood, mimicking Werner's posture by peering down her nose. She waggled a finger at an imaginary display case and pressed a fist into her hip. "You need to put your strong cheeses," she imitated his whine perfectly, "your Limburgers and Bleus off to one side so my Emmentaler," she clutched her chest dramatically, "doesn't pick up strange odors." I giggled.

"And he's getting crazier about getting sick." She plopped beside me which made her curls bounce. "You know how he stays an arm's length away from everyone?"

I nodded, remembering how he stepped away from her once she'd moved that puppy. The useless eater Werner had called it. That's where I'd heard the word recently. Useless.

"Now he's so afraid of getting sick," she continued, "that he drinks a health tonic every morning and takes cod liver oil and a dozen vitamins. He's taken to sleeping with a mustard plaster on his chest and a hat on his head."

"I'd like to get a picture of that!" I said, laughing.

Rennie grinned, her expression conspiratorial. "Have you ever seen him when someone coughs or sneezes?"

"I don't think so. What does he do?"

"This." She stood, drew a sharp breath, and lifted her hands to cover her face. Then she bent at the waist, made wet spitting sounds, and rushed to a pretend sink. There she cupped her hands and lifted them to her face over and over, spluttering. Then she rubbed her hands together and wrung them repeatedly.

"All because of a sneeze?" I couldn't stop laughing at her antics.

"A sneeze or a cough. Sometimes he even changes his clothes." That got us started in another round of giggles. "It's a good thing he doesn't do that while he's on duty as Youth leader. I can't imagine fifty boys splashing their faces when someone sneezes."

I shook my head. "I don't understand."

"The boys do what he does, like he's the Pied Piper of Hamelin."

I remembered the story. When the Piper played on his magic flute, rats poured out of homes and followed him. If the Piper turned, the rats turned. If the Piper stopped, the rats did too. Eventually, the Piper led the rats to a cliff where they fell off and drowned.

Rennie continued in a softer voice. "Can I tell you another secret?" Again I agreed. "I've thought about ways to change that story. Rewrite it." I waited while she focused her thoughts. "A rat could bite the Piper's ankle so he couldn't walk. Or break the pipe so it doesn't play." A small smile twitched at the corner of her mouth. "Or maybe the whole pack of rats could turn on the Piper and push him off the cliff."

I was surprised. Usually Rennie spoke so kindly.

She seemed embarrassed. "Horrid, I know." Her silver eyes searched my face expectantly. "But I do think that sometimes. It makes me wonder how he'll be after he goes through the Adolf Hitler School." The school provided training for young men to become Schutzstaffel, elite SS officers.

"I didn't know he applied."

She nodded. "It's a good place for him. He'd never make it in the trenches with the Wehrmacht. Too messy." I had to agree. "But the school will give him more training on how to make people follow. That's what I don't like." She patted my hand. "Your turn."

"My turn for what?"

"Tell me a secret."

My eyes darted to the pine trees and Rennie followed my gaze. "What? What's there?" I remained silent, unsure if I should share that particular secret with anyone. Her voice tinged with hurt, she whispered, "Don't you trust me?"

I shifted a little and turned to her. "Aside from my mother, I never told anyone."

She glanced at the trees and then back at me. "Told anyone what? Come on, Sophie. You can trust me."

That was true. Rennie was a good secret keeper. But I didn't know what she'd think of me once she heard the story. I glanced around to make sure I wouldn't be overheard, then leaned closer and whispered, "It's about Esther Kauffman."

Rennie's eyebrows pulled together. "The Jewish girl from our class? Didn't she move?"

I nodded. "When we were ten or eleven."

Rennie turned to me, her silver eyes intent on mine, her whisper a match for my own. "What about her?"

I drew my knees to my chest and wrapped my arms around them. Protected like that, I took a deep breath and began. "Our backyards faced each other, so Esther and I played together often when we were little. We especially liked playing spy, looking for clues to something or other." Rennie nodded, either

28

remembering that fact or encouraging me to continue. "A couple years before they moved, the SA stationed an armed guard outside Herr Kauffman's tailor shop because they were Jewish. His customers, even the loyal ones, were frightened away. His business dried up. The Kauffmans couldn't afford to stay there and had to move."

"You must have been sad to see her go."

I shrugged. "Yes and no." I lowered my head and spoke to the ground. "The SA scared me, with their uniforms and their guns. Plus I heard rumors about the Jews..." I chanced a brief look at Rennie and searched her face. Seeing no reaction, I dropped my gaze again. "I didn't want anyone to know I had a Jewish friend. I was afraid I'd get in trouble. So I made sure we played indoors or in the courtyard behind our homes where no one would see us."

It was probably only a few seconds before Rennie spoke, but it felt like an eternity. Her voice was soft. "Did you get to say goodbye?"

I nodded. "The night before they moved. Esther and I agreed to keep in touch with notes stuffed in a pickle jar and buried at the base of those trees." I pointed. "When we were younger, we dug for clues there during our spy games, so we both knew the place." I tipped my head toward Rennie and was glad to see a small smile there. "She and her father were just moving to the other side of Munich, so she expected to come here to the park from time to time."

Rennie turned to me. "And your friendship with her would stay secret."

I nodded. I wanted to ask her what she thought about that, if she'd still be my friend after this confession. Clearly it showed that I wasn't a true friend, one who would stand by steadfastly. But somehow, this story had unplugged a dam and my words wouldn't stop until all had poured out.

"The day they moved was the day our Jungmädel troop toured the Residenz Palace." Rennie made a "Hmm" sound. She remembered the day, so I continued. "We walked single file to the Palace, all of us in our uniforms and Anna in the lead. We went right past the Kauffman's shop.

"When we got close, Esther and her father were loading bags into a truck. They both waited, watching us. Someone at the front of our line sniggered and called them names. Maybe it was Anna, maybe one of the girls. I never knew because I was at the end of our line. Anyway, as I passed Esther, our eyes met. She took half a step toward me as if to reach out and hug me one last time." I closed my eyes and pictured Esther's silent expression, her dark eyes pleading for connection, for caring, for the friendship that had once been ours. My voice caught. "But I walked right past her. I was ashamed to show our friendship in public."

Long silent moments passed and I peeked over at Rennie. She brushed the back of her hand across her eyes. "I knew Esther from school," she said. "I could have stopped to say goodbye, too. So you're not the only one."

I shook my head. "You and Esther barely knew each other, but she and I were friends. I should have stood by a friend." After a few shuddering breaths, I pushed on. "In those first months, we stayed in touch with notes in the pickle jar and she never mentioned how hurt she must have been. I shared news from our neighborhood – a new baby down the street, someone going on a trip, a film I'd seen at the cinema, that kind of thing. Her notes were different, sad and frightened. She wasn't allowed in school anymore, and her father had to sew everything by hand since the Party took his sewing machine." I shook my head. "He didn't make much money. They had to share an apartment with other Jews, people they didn't even know, just to make ends meet. Every time I read one of her notes..." I stopped to focus my thoughts.

"We wrote regularly, probably once a week, placing the notes in the jar when we could." I closed my eyes again and tried to hold my breath steady. "One day, I noticed she hadn't picked up my last note. Another week or two went by, and it was still there. I began to worry. When a month passed and that note was still there, I was afraid for her.

"So I told my mother everything and asked her what to do. She was horrified. She said I could get in trouble for having a Jewish friend. She told me to concentrate on pulling up my mathematics grades and forget about Esther and silly notes." I sniffed. "How could I forget?" I lowered my legs, propped my elbows on my knees and leaned my forehead onto my hands.

Rennie's hand rested on my shoulder. "When was the last time you checked for a note?"

I shrugged. "Probably a year ago."

"Do you want to look now?"

31

I nodded slowly and, after making sure we were unseen, I led her to the spot. I scraped a stick across needles and soft earth which stirred up a sharp piney scent. Once the stick hit a hard surface I tossed it aside, scrabbling through the loose soil with my bare hands. When I'd cleared enough metal lid and glass to grab, I wiggled and tugged and pulled out the jar. Small globs of dirt spattered us. I twisted off the lid and pulled out the lone folded paper, musty and wrinkled. "This is the last note I wrote." I showed it to Rennie. "We always signed with initials, just S and E. Part of our spy games."

Rennie stared at the jar, its empty interior and its outside clotted with dirt. She shuddered. "It's spooky, isn't it? I mean, where did..." her words trailed off.

I responded slowly. "At first, I liked to think they were traveling on holiday, or maybe they'd left the country – I'd heard of other Jewish families doing that. But I've heard rumors, I guess we all have, about Jews going to work camps." I stopped speaking and Rennie didn't ask any more questions.

A few minutes passed and I stood, stretching my aching legs and back. "I don't need this anymore." I crumpled my old note and threw it in an overflowing bin several meters away. Rennie shoved the empty jar back in the hole and started to bury it, but I interrupted her. "I'll throw the jar out too."

Those dark curls of hers bobbed in a hopeful question. "What if Esther comes by someday? Don't you want some way for her to get a message to you?"

I hesitated but eventually agreed. I guess it wasn't risky, not really, and it did help me feel less guilty.

Since I'd already gone this far I forged ahead. "I hope you don't think poorly of me for telling you the biggest secret of all." Rennie's eyes widened and I gulped. "When these horrible things happened to Esther, I was sad for her. But I was awfully glad they didn't happen to me."

There. I said it.

Rennie hugged me. We sat in silence for a long, long time.

# Chapter Three
## Shadows

## 25 April, Monday

I gobbled dinner, changed into my BDM uniform, and hurried downstairs. Klaus waited there in his starched brown HJ uniform, his blond hair wet combed and his eyes bright as a spring morning. "We'll be home after the activity," he called to our mother, then stepped onto Reichenbach Strasse without waiting for a response.

I followed him. "So where are we going?"

"To meet up with other Youth."

"Where? What will you be doing? What am I taking pictures of?"

Klaus clucked his tongue. "You'll photograph whatever the Scharführer wants you to photograph."

"But I like to plan my shots..."

He flashed a smile my way. "Of course you do. You like things predictable and safe. Otherwise you'll just skitter off like the cat you are." I gulped. He faced forward again and gazed at something only he could see. "I like the challenge of split second reactions."

"Maybe that's why you're a good boxer." And a nasty fighter.

Another smile. "That's my dream. To be a world-class boxer."

"I thought you wanted to be a doctor."

He shrugged. "Maybe. For now, I just want to box."

It was hard to keep up with his ever-changing dreams.

He cut his eyes to me. "What about you, little cat? What's your dream?"

I didn't trust him with anything that intimate. "I want to get better at photography."

"Tell me something I didn't know," he said, chuckling.

I was still weak and achy from that lingering flu, but I did my best to match his long strides, the oversized camera bag bumping my hip. We stopped in a narrow street behind our old grammar school. The brick building had been an empty shell for a year or so since the Party closed it. I wondered where Sister Immaculata and the other nuns of the parish had gone. They were better teachers than those at my new Party-approved school.

A dozen or so Youth in uniform clustered in the street. Erich was there, and he gave me a small smile. My heart pounded.

"Most of you know my stepsister Sophie." Klaus poked his thumb toward me. "She'll photograph our," he snickered, "our activity later tonight for the newsletter." A sly smile spread across his face, one that I knew meant trouble. He turned to me. "Wait here. No photos yet."

Even if my camera had been ready, I wouldn't have been quick enough to photograph everything that happened next. Boys picked up rocks. Threw them at our old school. Glass shattered and crashed. Again. And again. Boys whooped. Reached through jagged edges of windows. Unlatched and pushed frames upward and climbed into the dark school.

My heart jumped and raced and my breath tried to catch up. But my body stood frozen.

Klaus. Why would my stepbrother vandalize our grammar school? And Erich. Where was he? I'd lost sight of him when the first window broke.

Footfalls, crashes, and shouts echoed through the empty building. In no time, the boys climbed through the shattered windowpanes, raised fists holding booty.

Crucifixes.

Brass crosses high and glinting in the late day sun, the boys raced down the street, hollering. Horror poured lead into my legs. Klaus gestured for me to follow. I didn't, I couldn't. He grabbed my elbow and dragged me along, stumbling and silent. Ahead of us, Erich ran with the pack.

When the boys hopped on a streetcar, Klaus practically had to lift me up beside them. I sat staring at my fingernails, out the window, anywhere but at the loud and rowdy boys with their shiny prizes. I definitely couldn't look at Erich.

As we neared the Haus der Deutschen Kunst, the art museum, Klaus tugged my arm and we followed the boys off the streetcar. They fell into formation and paraded, right arms raised in salute, past the Party guards posted at the museum, then broke off and raced each other into the English Garden Park. Klaus' firm pressure pulled me after them.

We reached an empty field where a brass crucifix had been propped against each of a dozen thin trees. The boys stood at attention in front of the pacing figure of the Scharführer. Klaus released my arm and fell into place beside them.

"Ah, here's our photographer, at last," Werner whined. "Come, come. Don't be afraid, Adler. Photograph our excellent Youth during their target practice. Show their camaraderie, their focus, their intensity, and their joy." He raised an eyebrow and continued. "Don't show the targets. The targets are," he hesitated, "unimportant." He gave each boy a handgun.

Crucifixes used for target practice. My heart pounded and my hands shook as I obediently opened the large bag and lifted the camera.

"*Eins.*" The boys stiffened.

"*Zwei.*" The boys raised their guns and took aim.

"Adler," Werner scolded, "You aren't ready."

He was right. I wasn't ready. Not with my camera, not with my thoughts, not with any part of me. I took a deep breath and glanced around quickly. "Excuse me *bitte*, I'm on the wrong side for the photo. I need to stand over there," I pointed to the other side of the line of boys, "with the sun at my back."

"*Ja, ja.*" He waved a hand. "*Schnell!*"

The boys froze in their ready pose while I hurried behind them. Erich's eyes followed me part of the way, but I couldn't think about him. I refocused my camera, checked my lighting, and nodded to Werner.

"*Drei.*"

Waves of deafening blasts pounded my ears and I stiffened against the jarring force. Click.

Again and again, noise assaulted me, metallic pings, dull thuds, triumphant shouts. I trembled, but I focused. Click. Click.

Steady hands on guns. More blasts. Click.

Smoke at gun barrels. Concentration etched on faces. Click.

Just the boys. No targets. Click.

My nostrils burned, my aching ears buzzed, and my head throbbed. Thankfully, one by one, the boys lowered their smoking weapons.

If I hadn't been assigned to photograph the event, I know what I would have done – run home at the first sign of this sacrilege. But I'd mustered up the courage to stay and finish my assignment.

I glanced at the camera. Two exposures left. I started to pack up when white chalky smudges on the sharkskin caught my attention. Papa's floury fingerprints. "Photograph the truth," he'd told me. "The whole truth."

So this is what Papa meant. The dented crosses, the spent shells told the whole truth. I could capture that in two photos, as I'd promised. Now that would take real courage.

Erich walked over. "You have film left?" I noticed his hands trembling. From excitement? Fear?

"A couple shots."

Then Werner's voice was behind me. "Then you'll photograph the first aid demonstration for our Youth newsletter." He pressed his fists to his hips and shifted his gaze from the camera to my face, waiting.

What else could I do? I tucked the camera in its case and snapped the bag shut. But the back of my throat thickened. I'd just broken a promise to Papa. I was one of those cowards Papa talked about.

The boys followed their Pied Piper to an adjacent field and Klaus grabbed my elbow to hurry me after them. My heavy legs slowed us, but eventually we caught up.

A number of boys were bent over a small stream, rinsing their hands and faces, playfully splashing one another and laughing. Some collected wood and tended the beginnings of a campfire. Others pulled bandages, wraps, and ointments from rucksacks. Their voices were soft, their manner civilized as if the vandalism, looting, and gunfire never happened. The stunning change made my head pound.

We found Werner beside the campfire. "It's getting late, and I didn't bring a flash," I told him. "So I'll go home." I wanted to go to bed and forget the whole horrible evening.

But he'd have none of it. "You'll stay until Klaus is done. We can't have young girls on the streets alone. Too many ruffians."

From somewhere behind me, Erich appeared. "I can walk Sophie home." He looked at his shoes and then up at the Youth leader, but not at me.

"*Nein.* Your place is here with your fellow Youth. Adler can wait for her brother." He shooed Erich with a wave of his hand. "Back to work." Erich looked at me, tipped his head sideways in silent apology and did as he was told. "Besides, Adler," Werner said, "photographers from all over Europe will be here tonight. You could learn from them."

I plopped near the campfire and jammed a stick at it. On its own, a muscle in my calf twitched and jumped. I squeezed it a few times to make it stop. That headache was working its way up and over my skull. I closed my eyes and tried to think about something else.

Members of the press corps, six or seven in all, trickled in and introduced themselves to Werner and the boys. A thin Italian with a fantastically large camera around his neck, a high-strung Frenchman who jumped every time the fire crackled, others whose nationalities and faces blended in the fading daylight. A rather short man limped over, knocking his bowler hat askew with each lurching step. "Peter Massey," he said, shaking hands all the way around. "Sorry I'm late. Don't walk as quickly as you."

Werner shifted into his formal announcement tone. "Let's begin. A nation's youth is its future. Germany builds its future by building a Youth that's strong and ready to serve at a moment's notice. Therefore, all HJ and BDM members are taught first aid." He gestured to various stations where boys simulated injuries. "Our older members will demonstrate some basics of emergency care."

The press moved from one cluster of boys to the next, photographing, grumbling about the fading daylight, and leaning toward the fire as they scratched notes onto a pad. One asked what was so special about kids' first aid practice and another shrugged his response.

Peter Massey stopped when he noticed me. "You're the only young lady here." I could tell by his accent that he was British.

"Waiting for my stepbrother."

He gestured toward the oversized camera bag at my feet. "Yours?"

I nodded. "I don't have a flash."

"You're welcome to use mine."

"That's very kind." I rose and stretched out my hand. "Sophie Adler."

His smile was friendly, genuine. "Are you related to Hans Adler, the owner of the bakery on Reichenbach Strasse?"

I smiled. "That's my father."

Herr Massey smiled. "We use the same photo studio in Schwabing. I've met your father there a few times." I warmed at the mention of my father and the studio. "And of course," he patted the roundness of his stomach, "I've sampled his crullers."

With his guidance, I adjusted my settings and used the flash for the last two photos, one of the boys placing an arm in a sling and another of them dressing a fictitious leg wound. "*Danke*, Herr Massey."

He tipped his hat. "Always glad to help a fellow photographer. *Guten Abend*, Sophie Adler." He limped out of the ring of firelight until all I saw was his lurching shadow.

My mother sat in her wing chair, peering at me over her spectacles. She pressed the back of her hand to my forehead. "Ach, you have that flu again. I told you to rest and you didn't. That's what you get."

The twitch in my calf had gotten worse. Without bothering to wash up or comb out my braids I stumbled to my room, pulled on a gown, then crawled under my quilt. In fifteen minutes, the muscle twitch grew into a toe-curling charley horse, so I repositioned my legs. My shoulder cramped so I fluffed my pillow. The pain from my throbbing head spread down the back of my skull, grabbed my neck, and held it stiff.

The bedroom door opened and Mutti bustled in carrying a speckled enamel washbasin. "In case you vomit," she announced, setting it down with a clatter.

I must have dozed off because I awoke cold and shivering. I tried reaching for my quilt but couldn't grab hold of it. When I pushed up to see what was wrong, strange sensations overwhelmed me – pain, melting. I tumbled from the bed like a rock from a cliff and struck my face on the floor. My hands hadn't broken my fall.

Warm wetness leaked from my nose. I tried to move but my arms cramped and wouldn't push. I couldn't even lift my head. My neck was stuck in place, stiff, too painful to move. Chills made me shiver, and that worsened the muscle cramps. As if pulled by an invisible string, my right knee bent so my heel nearly touched my backside.

I was powerless against whatever force had taken over my body. Terror washed over me and overwhelmed my thoughts. I tried to call for help, but I could barely pull in enough breath. "Mutti!" I croaked. Again. Again.

My mother rushed in, wrapping a robe around her floral nightgown. I must have looked a fright, flat on the floor with a bloody face and one leg jackknifed. She froze in the doorway and stared. At her heels, Klaus gasped. "Sophie," my mother whispered, advancing slowly toward me. "What's happened?" She knelt beside my bent leg and slowly ran her hands along its contour. "Can you stand?"

"No. Hurts." I could barely catch my breath. "So weak. And cold."

She pressed an icy hand to my forehead, and her eyes widened in alarm. "Get Herr Doktor Vogel," she told Klaus. "Tell him your sister is feverish. And weak. And there's something wrong with her leg."

"But it's nearly midnight," Klaus protested.

She glared at him. "He's an old friend of her father's. He'll come."

She placed a pillow beneath my head and clamped off my bloody nose. Then she draped a quilt over me and sat beside me on the floor. Once or twice, she even patted my hand. I should have been amazed at her attempts at tenderness, but I was too miserable to care.

Doktor Vogel did the usual. He listened to my chest, took my temperature, and asked about my symptoms. Then he did some unusual things. "Touch your chin to your chest." I tried but pain in my back and neck made me cry out. "Does this hurt?" He squeezed the fleshy parts of my legs and I yelped my answer. He took his spectacles off and turned to my mother. "It's probably infantile paralysis. Polio. She has all the symptoms." He gazed at me, his eyes filled with pity.

Polio. I knew what polio was. Everyone knew. First, a little cold or flu hung on too long. A high fever followed, and that's when the real problems started. Breathing problems. Possible death.

People who survived were left with weak muscles. Even after months of grueling therapy, weakness was still there. Sometimes a little. Sometimes a lot. Some people were left completely paralyzed.

If I lived through this, I was going to be crippled. It couldn't be true. It just couldn't.

Doktor Vogel stuffed his stethoscope in his bag. "It's been a bad season for polio. Sophie's the second this week." Then he turned to me. "I'll see you at the hospital."

The hospital? My grandfather died in a hospital.

# Chapter Four
# Blurred

I was flat on my back, a passenger on a bed. I couldn't turn or sit or even draw enough breath to ask the orderlies where I was going. Glaring lights appeared and disappeared overhead at regular intervals. I counted them, seventeen, just to do something, anything, to get my mind off the unending muscle cramps. I shivered uncontrollably.

Doors banged open and I was pushed into a darkened place. My movement stopped. The orderlies walked to a well lit area in the far corner of the huge room. They spoke in hushed tones with two women in white uniforms, gesturing toward me. All wore face masks.

My nose twitched at the room's strong odors. Rubbing alcohol and urine. Something else demanded my attention, a noise, a rhythmic whoosh, loud and mechanical. Whoosh-shhhh. Whoosh-shhhh. The sound filled the room.

I strained to see its source. A bed-height metal tube, wide and long, dotted with knobs and dials. Sticking out of the end of the tube was – I gasped – a child's head.

I had to get away. I tried to move, to sit up, scream, run, anything. Pain and weakness and lack of breath tethered me to the bed.

The orderlies reappeared. They pushed me past several beds and their lumpy inhabitants toward the whooshing tube. I tried to scrabble away, twisting this way and that against my spasms. I would not let them to push me into that metal monster.

My bed stopped beside the tube, and the orderlies abandoned me there. I wanted to be anywhere except in this aching, twitching body, alone with that horrid machine.

But as I lay there beside that tube, something odd happened. The rhythm of the whoosh lost its threat. It was predictable, dependable, and I soon found my labored breath matching its pace. In. Out. In. Out. I relaxed a bit. That's when I dared a closer look at the tube and the child inside.

It was Trudi, the little girl from my Jüngmadel troop.

My scrabbling started anew. I clawed and thrashed against my pain, against my horror and panic.

A man in street clothes approached. Doktor Vogel's clear blue eyes were recognizable above his white mask and I searched them for help, for hope. He pulled out his stethoscope and pressed its cold bell against my chest.

I managed to croak, moving my eyes toward the tube. "Trudi."

He nodded and spoke in the measured doctor voice he used for official business. "She's in an iron lung. When someone is too weak to breathe, the machine breathes for them."

I concentrated on each breath. In. Out. In. Out.

Doktor Vogel draped the stethoscope around his neck. His eyes and his voice were soft. "You're in the isolation ward, Sophie. Polio's contagious, and everyone must be protected. Even the nurses and staff wear masks so they don't catch it."

"All these patients have polio," he continued. I glanced around the darkened ward, its dozen or so patients silent and unmoving. "No visitors allowed. Once you've moved into the rehabilitation ward, your family and friends can visit."

A nurse rolled me, washed me, and tucked my sheets beneath the mattress. I was bread dough, kneaded, folded over, and stuffed into a pan.

I might die. I'd definitely be crippled. And there was nothing I could do about it.

A pat on my hand aroused me. Above the hovering face mask, a woman's deep green eyes showed concern. "How are you feeling, Sophie? Better?"

It took a few moments to remember – I was in the hospital. Every muscle in my body ached; I was one big charley horse.

"You gave us quite a scare." Her voice was familiar.

Doktor Vogel leaned over the other side of my bed and listened to my chest, then propped his elbows on the bedrail. "Your fever spiked yesterday and you didn't respond for seventeen hours. Breathing troubles." He regarded me intently. "I thought you might need the iron lung, but thankfully you didn't." That empty metal tube sat near my bed, silent.

I tried to speak, to ask about Trudi, but my breath caught. I had to concentrate to keep it going. In. Out. In. Out.

He continued. "Thank God you didn't need to go in the iron lung. Don't misunderstand – it's a wonderful

47

device, and it saves lives. But once used, it's hard to remember how to breathe on your own."

I pulled in a painful breath and on the exhale, I made some noise that sounded enough like "Trudi" that they understood I was asking about her. The woman's eyes dropped, but Doktor Vogel's gaze was steady. "She died last night, Sophie."

## 2 May, Monday

When I awoke, that woman with eyes the color of pine needles greeted me. She was rather tall and her bun sat like a cinnamon roll at the back of her head. "Hello, Sophie."

I blinked a few times. "Anna?" My old Jungmädel leader?

Small crinkles formed around her eyes. "*Ja*, it's me. I've started my nurses' training. This is my first rotation. You're my assignment for the next six months."

Six months?

She must have seen the surprise in my face. "Well, I'll be here for six months," she corrected, sounding positively excited. "You're one of the patients I'll follow. From hospital to rehabilitation unit and right through discharge."

Those eyes of hers searched my face, and her tone shifted from friendly to prying. "Strange how you and Trudi both ended up with polio, but no one else from the troop has it. Why is that?"

That's when it hit me. I'd gotten sick from sharing my canteen with Trudi. She was contagious and didn't know it.

I hoped I hadn't given it to anyone else.

I didn't answer Anna though. She'd only scold me, tell me I should have known better. And that wouldn't change anything. Trudi would still be dead. I would still be sick.

The best way to deal with Anna was the way I'd always dealt with her - stay hidden in the background, out of her focus. And I'd thought my days of dealing with her were over.

Luckily, our conversation was interrupted. A woman with cropped hair and an athletic build lugged a tall mirror across the room and stood it near my bed. "I'm Gisela." Her mask muffled her cheerful voice. "I'm a physiotherapist. I hear your muscle pain has lessened."

I nodded. Thankfully, I was able to breathe and move my arms a little without too much pain.

"Let's try a few exercises to see if you're ready to be transferred." While Anna stood by with her arms crossed, Gisela slid one hand under my shoulders, the other under my knees, and in a single smooth lift, sat me on the edge of my bed. She sat beside me, her arm around my shoulder for support.

I looked in the mirror. Next to Gisela sat a pale girl whose blonde hair was matted and clumped against her skull. The girl was thin, sickly thin, with rag doll arms and limp dangling legs. I knew I was the girl, but I didn't look like me.

"First we practice sitting." Gradually Gisela lessened her support at my shoulders, which left me to sway and bob until she steadied me. "Watch yourself in the mirror. It'll help you balance." Gisela released the support; I wobbled this way and that. Over and over.

49

Gisela smiled at my efforts, nodding. "Need a rest?" Without waiting for an answer, she scooped up my legs and lowered me to the bed. I grunted as clenched muscles in my neck and back uncurled, slowly releasing their hold on my spine. "Now roll onto your stomach please."

I moved my arms a little to start the roll and tried to do as she asked. My left leg helped some, but my right leg was completely limp. It didn't work, as if nothing connected my thoughts to my leg.

Anna continued to watch as the physio helped roll me, arranging and untangling my floppy limbs. "Now pretend you're swimming. Lift your arms and your legs, one, two, one, two."

My arms moved a little and my left leg moved some. My right leg lay on the bed as if made of lead. "I don't think I'm much of a swimmer. More like a dead fish." I buried my face in the mattress.

"Nonsense. You did well for your first try. I'll recommend you go to rehabilitation tomorrow to start some intensive physiotherapy. We'll work together twice a day."

"At what?"

"Getting you as strong as you can be."

"What about my right leg?"

"I don't know, Sophie." Gisela's voice softened. "Most everyone with polio gets strength back, sometimes a lot of it."

"How long will I have to do this therapy?"

She shrugged. "Can't say exactly. Most of our patients stay a few months and then go home. But be prepared. Exercising with polio hurts, and it'll be the hardest work you've ever done."

No one could predict how paralyzed I'd be. I'd be working hard with no end in sight. There was no way to make a plan. But I was better off than poor Trudi. I was alive.

## 3 May, Tuesday

I smoothed a blanket over my spindly legs as Anna pushed my wheelchair out of the hospital wing and down a long corridor. As we passed through some swinging doors, she faced me. "This can go now." She removed her mask and tossed it in a nearby bin.

I stared at her upturned nose, the soft point of her chin, and the small creases like parentheses around her mouth. I hadn't seen those familiar features since before my illness. As I entered this new stage of recovery, I liked the idea that someone I knew would be by my side. But I was still a bit nervous that the someone was Anna.

We entered the rehabilitation wing and she pushed me straight to the cafeteria. After a week of lying in bed surrounded by white walls, whispered voices, and the whoosh of the iron lung, the cafeteria was a colorful, active, and most welcome change.

The air was filled with happy chatter and scented with cinnamon and coffee. Two or three uniformed staff members fed little ones in high chairs. A dozen or so patients in street clothes, children, teens, and adults, sprinkled the large room. Some ate at tables, others walked with wooden crutches, and a few pushed themselves in wheelchairs. Many wore metal braces with brown leather strap supports, a couple had bracing on their torsos, and one boy's spindly arm lay strapped to a board.

Anna pushed me into an open spot at a table where four patients were already eating. A man with dark hair, probably in his twenties, spoke first. *"Grüß Gott.* I'm Herr Franken."

I wondered if he'd correct the mistake he'd made, using the traditional Bavarian greeting "God's greeting" instead of *"Heil Hitler."* But he just sat there smiling, waiting, so I responded in kind.

The others introduced themselves – Fritz, a grinning six-year-old, Marla, a quiet pale girl maybe eleven or twelve years old with shoulder length brown hair, and a pretty blonde teen named Elisabeth.

Anna placed a breakfast tray in front of me. At the hospital, I'd been spoon fed every meal as if I were a baby. I'd been as weak as one. Here in rehabilitation, I'd learn to do more for myself.

I reached for the spoon, but my fingers couldn't close around the handle. Anna's hand clasped over mine and she helped me scoop a bit of yoghurt and raise it to my mouth.

Eating demanded my full concentration so I didn't hear much of the conversation at the table. After a dozen spoonfuls, my arm shook with fatigue. Anna and I excused ourselves.

The pea green rehabilitation ward room was as large and open as the hospital ward with tall windows and a high ceiling. A console radio stood in a corner with a few chairs clustered around it. The eighteen or twenty beds on the ward looked just like the ones in the hospital, the white metal frames, crisp sheets, and gray wool blankets. But here, a few beds were spread with multi-colored knit afghans or puffy quilts, personal touches which made me smile.

Anna pushed me to a bed, lifted me in, and tucked the sheet around me. "Rest a bit." She started to leave.

I called after her. "Why are the other beds empty?"

She turned. "The patients are at breakfast or in therapy. The ward's pretty quiet during the day."

"When can I get my own things from home?"

"Your mother brought clothes a few days ago, a large bundle. You can open it after you rest."

Things were looking up. "When can I get a real bath and wash my hair?"

Anna crossed her arms, probably trying to look stern. "In an hour or so. Now, Sophie, you got tired eating breakfast. You need some rest."

But I wasn't done yet. "When do visitors come?"

"Saturday afternoons." She softened. "Your mother and your stepbrother are eager to see you. A few friends, also. Even the Scharführer has been asking for you."

I let my head sink into the pillow and smiled. People wanted to visit me. My eyes grew heavy, and I drifted into that pleasant, relaxed state that comes before sleep.

My eyes popped open. Werner wanted to visit?

Anna brought me to the physiotherapy room later that day. It was also a long rectangle, with the same tall windows and pea green walls as the ward. But instead of beds, it held a half-dozen padded tables. On one, a boy lifted his leg in the air and lowered it. On another, a woman on her hands and knees alternately arched her

53

back and let it sag. Across the room, children and adults pedaled stationary bicycles or tugged arm pulleys. Three women in white uniforms moved through it all, adjusting a sandbag here, helping someone sit there. Since one was Gisela, the other two must be physiotherapists too – physios they were called.

Gisela pushed me to an empty mat table and in moments, I was out of the wheelchair and on my back on the table. She took measurements and jotted notes. "Ready?" I nodded even though I didn't know what to expect. "Slide your legs out and in ten times. Then rest. Then another ten, and rest."

How many times she came and went, changing exercises or adding weights, I don't know. Maybe six, maybe a dozen. All I know is exercise made every muscle ache and quiver, and sweat drenched me.

After three quarters of an hour, Gisela said, "Good session. You're scheduled daily right after breakfast and then again mid-afternoon, two hours each."

"Two hours?"

"You'll learn to pace yourself. How do you feel?"

"Everything hurts. My legs and my back especially."

Gisela smiled. "That's normal, Sophie. Muscles hurt when they work. I'll stretch them out and your student nurse can give you a good massage later."

Slowly, with steady gentle pressure, Gisela lifted my arm. Pain tore at it as if fingernails raked and ripped at skin and muscles. Her expression was sympathetic and her voice soft, but I cried out a number of times anyway. When she was done I did feel better. But I was still trembling and sweaty.

Back at the ward, Anna spread a little talcum on her hands and rubbed my back. I was asleep in minutes.

That evening, she pushed me to the cafeteria and helped me with supper. She faced me, her expression stiff. "Well Sophie, I've given you all I could this week. I pushed you around, bathed you, fed you, and exhausted myself giving you backrubs. Time for me to go home." She turned on her heel and left.

Same old Anna.

Herr Franken watched her leave, a single eyebrow raised. He turned to me. "Evenings here are free time. Do whatever you like."

I'd like to play checkers with Papa, sing radio songs with Klaus, and have Mutti show me a new knitting pattern. But I couldn't. I was in a wheelchair, in the hospital with strangers.

Marla must have seen my uncertainty. "Last night was my first night over here. I went to the ward to listen to the radio."

"The radio has too many speeches," little Fritz said, scrunching up his face. Herr Franken tousled Fritz's head.

Marla looked down at her lap. "The speeches might be important."

Elisabeth flipped her long blonde braids over her shoulders. "Some people stay in the cafeteria to play cards. There are board games," she gestured to boxes on shelves behind me, "chess and *Mensch Ärgere Dich Nicht.*"

"That sounds fun," I said.

"And there are good books in the hospital library," Herr Franken chimed in.

"I like to read," I said. "I was reading books about photography before I got sick."

Fritz's blue eyes shone. "Do you have a camera?"

"What do you take pictures of?" Elisabeth sounded interested.

"I took pictures of a Youth activity a couple of weeks ago." A lifetime ago.

"What was it, a race?" Marla wanted to know.

"No." The memory of how I broke my promise to Papa that day gnawed at me.

"Well, the library's across from the physio room," Herr Franken said, "so come on down if you're interested. You too, Marla." He grabbed his wooden crutches and stood, slowly and with grunts, tucking the crutches into his armpits. He plodded across the cafeteria stiffly, his metal- and leather-bound legs improbable toothpicks under his adult body.

Marla pushed away alone. For only her second day in rehabilitation, she was getting around pretty well. Elisabeth stood with a single metal crutch, clamped it around her left forearm, and waddled off, blonde braids whipping from side to side like wipers on a windshield. She wore only one brace, a short one on her right leg. Fritz sat in his wheelchair watching me, then spun and pushed himself out of the cafeteria.

My muscles already ached from the day's therapy. I hadn't pushed the wheelchair myself and I didn't want to try. The only other person in the cafeteria was an elderly man holding a mop. He nodded at me and started his work.

It took me ten minutes to push from the cafeteria to the ward. But I did it.

The Führer's voice boomed from the ward radio and I pushed toward it, drawn by its magnetism, a familiar something amid the strangeness of the past days. I was barely inside the ward room when the broadcast was over, but several patients and two staff members still clustered near the radio, talking excitedly. Marla sat at the edge of the group, half-listening to them and half-watching my approach.

I pulled up next to her. "What did I miss?" I asked, out of breath. "Something important?"

Her eyes widened. "Well, of course it was important," she whispered, leaning close to me. "It was the Führer."

# Chapter Five
## Lighting

## 6 May, Friday

I studied the reflection at the end of the parallel bars – me in my wheelchair looking terrified, Gisela squatted beside me holding a roll of tan wrap and a flattened metal bar. "Are you sure that will hold me?" I asked.

"Not by itself, Sophie." She laid the bar across her lap, placed my limp leg on top of it, and with smooth V's from ankle to mid-thigh, wrapped them together. "This temporary brace, we call it a temp, will keep your right knee from buckling when you stand. Your arms and your other leg will do most of the work."

"But I pushed to the cafeteria this morning, then all the way here." I heard myself whine. "My arms are tired."

"I'll hold you. You won't fall, I promise."

Anna had been standing nearby, and now she placed a hand on my shoulder. "I'll stay close too."

What else could I do? In. Out. In. Out.

With grunts and tugs and a lot of help I stood upright, gripping the bars. Gisela used her shoe to push the wrapped leg back so it propped under me like a tripod under a camera. I peered past Gisela and caught a glimpse of my grimace. My image blurred.

"I'm going to slide your right leg forward," Gisela said, hooking her foot around my heel. "Let yourself down, easy now." I plopped in the wheelchair, exhausted and light-headed.

"Thirty seconds!" Anna sounded pleased.

"It had to be longer than that." I dropped my head to bring the blood back. If standing was this hard, how would I ever walk?

A few hours later I pulled up beside Elisabeth at a long black table in a place that was new to me, Occupational Therapy. Elisabeth dug at a piece of wood with a sharp tool. "What are you doing?" I asked.

"Carving a tree." She smiled at it admiringly. It looked like a gouged out hunk of wood to me.

Marla sat nearby, scowling at the lumpy blue web draped between her knitting needles. Fritz hollered a greeting as a blob of scarlet paint dripped from the brush in his hand. All through the room, patients hammered, cut paper, and folded towels. Not an exercise mat or a pulley in sight.

A stout, middle-aged woman bustled over. "I'm Frau Berkheimer, the Occupational Therapist. You must be Sophie Adler."

I nodded. "This therapy of yours looks different than physio."

Her smile was broad and proud. "It is. Here in OT, we strengthen your hands and keep your mind busy. What do you enjoy?"

"Taking pictures. Can you get me strong enough to work my camera?"

She stepped away and returned with her answer – a damp ball of clay, a rolling pin, and a butter knife.

"Flatten it, then cut long strips. Weave the strips together."

"Like a pie crust?" I pictured our bakery's pies with fruit bursting between woven bits of top crust. She nodded.

I flattened the ball a bit by pressing with my palms and flipping it over. Then I tried the rolling pin. I had to lean my forearms on it and rock back and forth to make enough pressure. In no time, my shoulders ached. I cut, lifted, wove, grasped, pinched, and tugged until my hands ached too.

Frau Berkheimer inspected my work. "Good. Now squash it back into a ball and do it again." I started to object but she raised a finger. I swallowed my complaint.

When I showed her my second woven creation, she took in the sweat on my forehead. "You're done. See you tomorrow."

No doubt about it. OT was just as hard as physio. The hard part was just better disguised.

An envelope addressed in unfamiliar handwriting waited on my bed.

*Dear Sophie,*

*I hear you've been sick. Klaus has kept me up to date and I'm glad to hear you're stronger now.*

*I had hoped to visit on Saturday, but I'll be away. My family is going to Kempten for my grandmother's birthday celebration. I'll plan to come another time.*

*Erich*
*P.S. When I visit, I'll bring a special surprise.*

I reread the note a dozen times, relishing the warm fluttery feelings it brought. I tucked it under my pillow and smiled the rest of the day.

## 7 May, Saturday

The ward doors swung open at 15 Uhr. A dozen visitors entered, their happy voices calling out to loved ones. Everyone walked right past me. I tugged my blanket to hide my scrawny legs.

A small boy climbed on Fritz's lap and begged, "Take me for a ride." The two of them zigzagged across the room, imaginary motor running and brakes squealing. A short couple stood nearby, beaming at them.

I moved to the windows to watch the adjacent parking lot for arrivals. Herr Franken joined me, clean-shaven and neatly groomed. Shortly, a young woman in a stylish dress and heels strode up the walk. "Ah, here's my Gabriele," he said, his voice a tender whisper. He lifted a hand from a crutch to wave. A huge smile lit the woman's face as she hurried into the building.

Herr Franken bowed to me and began his plodding steps. Gabriele never took her eyes from her husband's face as they walked toward each other, her arms outstretched in greeting, his hands grasping crutches to support his weight on withered legs. They walked slowly toward the outdoor patio, their faces shining.

Maybe I'd be loved that way. Someday.

A square woman in a calico housedress stepped off a streetcar. "Mutti!" I called, waving as she entered the ward. I was surprised how much I'd missed her.

61

She froze in the doorway. She looked me up and down and up again, then gazed around the ward, taking in the beds, the wheelchairs, the people. A sharp breath and then, "Which bed is yours?"

I pointed. She strode to it, plopped a paper-wrapped bundle and a couple of shopping bags beside it and turned, hands on hips, staring at everything and everyone.

Not the warm greeting I wanted. I gestured to a nearby chair. "Please sit so we can visit."

But she stood stock still and lifted her chin. "All these people have polio?"

"Yes."

My answer made wrinkles between her brows. She said, "Hmpf," then turned and went to work unpacking the parcel. In minutes, my dirty clothing was ready to go home and fresh blouses, camisoles, socks, and underwear were smoothed, refolded, and tucked in neat piles in my drawers.

I thanked her and peeked in one of the shopping bags. "My quilt!" Its tiny pink, blue, and yellow rosebuds spoke of home, of my real life. A wave of homesickness swept over me.

She pulled the quilt from the bag and smoothed it across my bed. That done, she perched on the arm of the chair, probably deciding whether to stay or run out the door. She pursed her lips. "Are you getting stronger?"

"Yes, I am. It's really hard, but..."

"Then work harder. The harder you work, the stronger you'll be."

"I am working hard," I sputtered. "I'm doing the best I can with..." I scrunched my eyes shut and didn't open them until I could hold back tears.

"When will you be better?"

My voice grew hard. "I am better. Much better. I nearly went into the iron lung."

"I know. The nurse told me when I phoned."

I stared at her. "You phoned?" We had a telephone in the bakery, but it was for business use. My parents never used it for private calls.

"Of course. I wasn't allowed to visit."

I smiled. Maybe she really did care about me.

She shifted on her little perch. "I got word to your father about your illness."

"I'll write him once I can hold a pencil."

As that sank in, her eyes widened briefly. She reached into a shopping bag. "He asked me to bring this." She pulled out a familiar black leather case.

My eager hands grabbed for my camera. I cradled it awkwardly and stroked its grainy surface.

She continued. "He sent a letter too," waving an envelope she'd pulled from a pocket.

"Open it for me, *bitte*, and hand me the note." Again, she seemed surprised, but she did as I asked.

The envelope's seal had already been broken.

*My dear Sophiela,*

*I hear you are sick and in hospital. I am most distressed by this. I want to see you with my own eyes and know that you are healing, but I cannot. All I can do is pray that, by the time you get this letter, you are on your way to recovery.*

*As we march, I take photos of the beautiful people and places of Austria, sometimes one or two rolls in a day. I want to show you places I have seen and tell you stories behind the photos.*

*I have asked your mother to bring your camera and some film to the hospital. Please take photos of things you do and people who help you. I hope to get a pass to come home at Christmas. We can share our photos then and tell each other all we've missed.*

*Since you will not have a flash or a tripod, do not worry about lighting or background. The truth of what happens around you is enough.*

*Your loving Papa*


As I reread the note, I could almost hear my father's voice. I pictured him stepping away from a line of grimy soldiers to photograph a fabulous Alpine landscape, some grazing goats, a handful of waving villagers. What a great adventure. I turned to my mother. "Papa mentioned film."

Her eyes darted around the room. "I was, um…" She fidgeted. "I was unable to get any."

My bossy, always-in-control mother was nervous. Was it this place? Was it me?

"Can you bring some next week?" I gestured around me. "I can't exactly buy it here."

A squeal at the ward door interrupted us. Rennie ran to me, arms flung wide, then stooped to squeeze my neck in a crushing embrace. "You're choking me," I said, laughing. I was unbelievably glad to see her.

"Oh, Sophie." She pulled away to look at my face. "I've been so worried about you."

Uta and Marie hung back in the doorway, sizing up the situation before they came over. They greeted my mother, and gave me brief sideways hugs and feather light pecks on the cheek. "How are you feeling?" Uta asked in an overly polite sort of way. She scanned me up and down, probably seeing just how crippled I was.

I was anxious to distract her. "You'll never guess who my student nurse is."

Uta and Marie looked at me blankly, but Rennie piped up. "It's Anna." The other two groaned when I nodded. "Werner told me."

"How did he know?"

"He and Anna are sort of seeing each other," she said.

Uta and Marie groaned again. "Nothing personal, Rennie," Marie said, "but I can't picture Werner with a girlfriend."

Uta shook her head. "I can't picture Anna *as* a girlfriend!"

"She's been nice to me since I've been here." I lowered my voice to a near whisper. "Sort of." My three friends nodded their understanding.

"We can only stay a few minutes, Sophie," Marie said. "We have to set up for a BDM meeting tonight."

Uta chimed in. "Marie and I are in charge of refreshments."

Rennie's curls bobbed as she plopped on my bed and faced me. "I can stay a while." She smiled her sweet, familiar smile. "I'm on clean-up."

Uta shifted. "Don't be late, Rennie. We have a lot of planning to do."

"What are you planning?" I asked.

Marie piped up. "Don't you remember? *Landdienst.* We leave June first."

I'd forgotten. If I hadn't been hospitalized, I'd be leaving for the *Landdienst* work program too. During the summer months, Youth in German cities left their homes to labor on farms. Helping with crops and animal care was good, honest work, and it kept German mouths full.

"I brought a treat." Mutti reached in a bag and pulled out a small, towel-covered basket of our bakery's cinnamon buns. We ate our fill of the sticky heaven.

I gestured to the two buns left in the basket. "May I offer these to my other friends? Hospital food is nothing like this." My mother nodded, so I called Marla and Elisabeth over, introduced them, and offered them the extra buns.

Marla's eyebrows furrowed. "Are you sure that's fair? I mean, there's not enough for everyone."

Elisabeth reached her hand in the basket, smiling. "I'll take one, *danke*." She gestured to nearby patients, chatting happily with their guests. "They don't seem to mind." She bit into a bun, "Mmm," icing smearing across her lips.

Marla snatched the last bun. We giggled at her guilty expression.

As they ate, Rennie chatted with them about sweets and favorite candies. Uta and Marie smiled politely but said little, glancing around often, obviously uncomfortable.

All the while my mother moved around my bed, smoothing the quilt, fluffing the pillow. At one point she caught my eye, making sure I noticed as she tucked something under my pillow. Before I could ask, she furrowed her eyebrows to indicate, "Not now." So I stayed quiet.

As Marla and Elisabeth left to see their own guests, a familiar voice boomed across the ward. *"Heil, Hitler."* A few people responded in kind.

Klaus. He strode over and patted my head. "Hello, little cat." He nodded to my friends. "Girls." He faced me. "Has Mutti told you about Hans and his, um, indiscretion?"

Our mother glared at him and drew herself up as tall as she could, barely reaching his collarbone. She poked her finger in his chest. "Shame on you, barging in here and speaking that way of my husband." Her face was red, and a little bit of spittle flew from the corner of her mouth.

Smiling, Klaus raised his hands in mock surrender. "It's a simple question."

But Mutti continued to snarl. "He has been most kind to you," she emphasized each syllable with that prodding finger, "raising you as his own since you were barely out of diapers. What he is doing ..." With those words, her voice caught. She stopped speaking and dropped her arm.

What was Papa doing? In. Out. In. Out.

Klaus waved a hand as if shooing a fly. "Here we are mother, you and I, doing everything. Helping the Fatherland, managing the bakery, delivering." He poked a thumb toward me. "Sophie can't help us. She can't even help herself." I drew a breath and heard Rennie gasp, too. He continued, "Hans can't help us. He's a hundred kilometers away, in trouble for..."

Mutti snatched the empty shopping bags off my bed and stomped out. She didn't even say *Auf Wiedersehen*. I was stunned. It all happened so quickly.

Klaus settled in the armchair and leaned back, hands linked behind his head and ankles crossed in front of him. Pleased and confident, as if he'd won a boxing contest.

That brought me to my senses fast. "You're so mean," I growled. "I can't help it that I'm…" I fought the urge to cry.

"Remember when you took photos at our Youth event?"

I gulped. As if I could forget.

"You got sick right after that, so I gave the film to the Scharführer. He'll stop by today to talk with you."

My voice sounded weak, even to me. "He will?"

Uta stood. "Let's get some air." My three friends left me alone with my stepbrother.

"On to other things." He sat upright, pulled a wrinkled paper from a pocket, and thrust it to me. "Does this look familiar?"

I blinked, stunned. It was the last note I'd written to Esther, the one I'd tossed in a bin in the park before I got sick. I searched the words now, desperately hoping they wouldn't reveal too much.

*Dear E,*

*This is all so confusing. I can't tell anyone how I feel. Maybe someday we can speak about it face to face.*

*Yours,*

*S*

Klaus furrowed his brows in exaggerated concern and tapped the paper. "So little cat, can you explain this?"

# Chapter Six
# Glare

I couldn't deny I'd written the letter. My stepbrother knew my handwriting. I stammered, "Where, where did you get this?"

"I found it fluttering through the park, that day you were doing math. Were you expecting someone?" He watched me for a reaction. "You have confused feelings for someone?"

Panic rose in me like mercury in a thermometer. In. Out. In. Out. "It's none of your business, Klaus," I managed.

He rested his elbows on his knees, leaning so close I could smell onions on his breath. "What kind of a fool do you take me for, Sophie? I know what you're up to." My gut clenched. "Your boyfriends will always be my business."

Boyfriends?

"Erich the Beautiful, you call him, right?"

It took a moment. Klaus thought Erich was E. I reread the letter quickly. Nothing there contradicted Klaus' thought. If I played along, my secret letters to Esther stayed secret. "I've always thought Erich is good-looking." No surprise there.

Klaus chuckled and reached the letter toward me again. "Do you want this? Maybe to tuck under your pillow so you can dream about him?" He lifted his hands to one cheek and fluttered his eyelashes. "Oh, Erich," he crooned.

My panic settled. Klaus didn't know a note in Erich's real handwriting was under my pillow. "Just put it in my drawer," I said. That was close.

My girlfriends hesitated in the doorway, so I waved them in. "I leave in a couple of weeks," Klaus said as the girls sat, "to start my time with the RLS." Young men around his age served their obligation in the Reich Labor Service by working for six months or so clearing land, draining swamps, big projects like that. After RLS, they began their military service.

"You'll all be gone." I choked on the bitter loneliness of my words.

Rennie tipped her head in silent apology. "We'll be back after the harvest. November probably."

Klaus turned to something outside the ward's windows then abruptly bolted out the door. Uta and Marie stood, peering outside on tip toe, but Rennie stayed right beside me. Good old Rennie.

Mutti was still out there waiting for the streetcar, talking with Werner and our BDM leader Helga. My mother's head turned repeatedly as first Werner and then Helga spoke. When Klaus arrived and placed himself beside the Youth leaders, Mutti scowled at him. She climbed on the arriving streetcar alone. Klaus and the leaders exchanged salutes and parted.

"What was that all about?" I mumbled, knowing full well my girlfriends didn't have the answer. Werner and Helga entered the ward, so I tucked the blanket around my legs.

71

Uta stood quickly. "Well, we really must be going. Wonderful seeing you, Sophie."

Marie did likewise. "Yes, glad you're feeling better." They stopped when the leaders entered, saluted their greeting, and raced to catch the streetcar.

I'd never thought much of it when people saluted. But saluting at the hospital felt wrong somehow, like shouting in church.

Werner tossed a bulky envelope into my lap. "We've come to see you about these photos." He kept his distance from me and eyed the other patients warily.

"I, I haven't got the strength," I whispered to Rennie, waggling my weak fingers.

She nodded, slid the stack of photos from the envelope, and lifted the first by its edges for my inspection. A full-length profile of a uniformed Youth member, his handgun aimed at an unseen target. Well focused. Good composition. Lighting adequate. She lowered it and raised the next, time and again, letting me examine them without comment. All stills; no action shots. Later, I'd match these results to the notes I'd jotted down. Overall, I was pleased.

But again I tasted acid, disappointment at my failure to capture the whole truth as I'd promised Papa – spent shells beside dented crucifixes.

Werner snatched the pile of photos and pocketed them. "I've shown these to other Youth Leaders. We've decided."

I reached out my empty hand. "I need to compare these photos to my notes…"

He ignored me. "You'll get two rolls of film a month while you are here in rehabilitation. Use the film to keep your skills sharp." He gazed around the ward. "You're confined here, yes?" I nodded. "Then you'll photograph this place and these people."

In a single afternoon, my camera and a supply of film had come to me!

"That way when you're discharged, you might still be of some use. Not like the rest of these," he waved his hand at the ward, "these useless eaters."

Same term he'd used for that deformed puppy. I wrapped my arms around my stomach.

Werner raised his voice so everyone in the ward could hear. "Yes, those who use German resources without giving back to the *Volk*, they're useless. At least you, Adler, you have a skill the Reich can use even though you're crippled."

In. Out. In. Out.

Helga spoke up. "Surely you realize the Reich is showing kindness, giving you a chance to contribute." She hesitated as if I ought to offer my thanks. When I didn't, she continued in her bored tone. "Since you can't keep up with the other girls, you won't be in BDM anymore."

"But," my voice squeaked, "I pledged. I'm the Youth photographer. My friends…"

Werner held up his hand. "We've told your mother. It's arranged."

The pledge ceremony and one awful activity, and my time in BDM was over. My thoughts were unfocused, blurry.

From a second pocket, he produced two small tins and set them on my dresser. "In a few weeks, I'll pick up this film. If your photos are," one corner of his mouth lifted, "approved, you'll be given two more rolls." He saluted and Helga echoed it. They both held the pose, waiting.

Rennie glanced at me and poked my right arm. I raised it a little, but I didn't look at the leaders. They must have been satisfied because they left.

I let my hand flop into my lap and closed my eyes, too stunned to speak.

"Let's get some air." Rennie rose and without waiting for a response, pushed me onto the porch. She flopped into a chair and barely held back tears. "He makes me so mad."

The catch in my voice matched the one in hers. "My own Youth leaders don't want me. They think I'm useless." We sat that way, each of us upset and sniffling, lost for a time in our own pain.

Gradually my senses stirred, as if harsh words and illness and the stuffy ward had been a bad dream. There before me, tiny brown birds hopped through manicured grass, scolding each other with soprano cheeps. A motor car approached, its tires grumbling along the cobblestone street. The sweetness of lilacs and geraniums surrounded me, filled me. Sunlight bathed my arms, its warmth seeping down to my bones, right to my soul.

While I'd been sick, life had continued.

Rennie patted my hand. "Tell me everything that's happened."

So I did, starting with the Youth activity the night I got sick right up until that very morning. When I was done, I said, "Wait right here." I pushed into the ward and returned a minute later, my lap piled with a notepad and pencil, my camera bag, and a tin of film. "Can you take dictation?"

Rennie grinned and settled back, pencil in hand. I chose my words carefully.

*Dear Papa,*

*I'm getting stronger all the time. I even stand a little with my temporary brace.*

*Today was my first visitation, and I had lots of company. Rennie is here now, writing this for me. Mutti brought my camera and your letter. The Scharführer brought film so I can keep up my photography skills.*

*I'll take lots of photos of the people here. I can't wait to show them to you and tell you all about this place and what we do here.*

*I hope you're enjoying Austria. Please write me again and tell me all about it. You can post your letter to me at the hospital.*

*I miss you, Papa.*

*Your Sophiela*

"Now," I said, giving her the camera clumsily, "I'd like help loading the film." She moved her fingers toward some white smudges on the leatherette. "Don't touch those," I said quickly. "They're Papa's fingerprints. Flour." She didn't need more explanation. Good old Rennie.

Step by step, I told her how to open the camera's hinged back and load the film on the spindles. I could only watch. Frustration at my own weakness filled me, and again I blinked away tears.

Once the film was loaded, I asked, "Can I take a photo of you?"

She leaned into me and hugged, her dark curls pressing my face. "I'd like that." She hurried to the porch railing where deep green hollies formed a perfect backdrop for her ivory skin.

To extend the bellows on my camera, I needed to press a tiny latch release no bigger than the nib of a pen, then grasp a lever with two fingers of my other hand and pull, all while stabilizing the camera. But instead of pressing, grasping, and pulling, my doughy fingers collapsed and slipped on the small mechanisms. I didn't just need help loading the film. I needed help working the camera. I was no photographer.

Rennie read my expression and hurried over. "It has a timer, right?" I nodded. Her gray eyes locked on mine, earnest. "We can do this." Gently, she worked the sticky latch and pulled open the thick folded bellows. "There. Let's get a picture of both of us." She brought a small table over and sat the camera on it. "You're the photographer," her voice was encouraging, "so you set up the shot. We'll set the timer together."

I slid the camera around the tabletop and asked her to pose again in front of the hollies. My thumbs didn't work for the fine buttons and latches, but they did work to spin the brass focus dial. "I need help with the shutter speed and the aperture." Again, she left her spot and moved the tiny indicators to the settings I chose. "See that lever with the red button?" I said. "Click it, then press the one with the notches. That'll give a fifteen second delay."

She shook her head. "We'll do it together."

I placed my clumsy pointer finger on the red lever, and she placed her sturdy finger on top of mine.

Together, we pressed the timer and then the shutter. Together, we hurried to the bushes and posed, smiling genuine smiles, as the shutter clicked.

That night as I slid my hands under my pillow, I felt for Erich's letter. Something else was under there too, a lumpy drawstring pouch. Rosary beads and a note in my mother's hand.

*Sometimes I'm followed. Perhaps our family is being watched. Be careful.*

My heart raced and I glanced around the ward room, checking to see if anyone's eyes were on me. I transferred to my wheelchair, pushed to the bathroom, and flushed the note down the toilet.

I said the rosary three times that night, but it didn't bring me comfort.

Now that I had my camera and film, I had a plan. I'd work extra hard in OT toward my goal of being a photographer again. And it worked. My arms got stronger, and I needed less help lathering a washcloth and combing my hair. I even pushed my wheelchair most places while Anna walked beside me. But sometimes, after a long day of therapy, I was drenched with sweat and my twitching, aching arms didn't have one push left. Anna would shake her head and say "Aww", as if I were an injured kitten. Then she'd push me to the ward to massage the aching knots in my muscles.

In physio, I grew strong enough to sit for three or four minutes and slide myself along a little board to get from my wheelchair to my bed. I even took a few steps in my temp in those long parallel bars. But my right leg still didn't move much. It hung down sort of limp, a cooked noodle draped over the side of a pot.

## 14 May, Saturday

Rennie and the other BDM girls had gone camping for the weekend. I pictured them roasting wieners over a fire, singing songs, and hiking mountain trails while I sat there in the hospital, in a wheelchair. When large raindrops speckled the pavement and splashed the windowpanes, part of me, a mean but honest part, hoped the girls were stuck inside their tents.

Mutti entered the ward room at full speed, performed her visual inspection of her surroundings, and tipped her nose to show her disapproval. Then she kissed the top of my head – an actual kiss! – and lowered her square frame to my bed. Her gaze fell to my spindly right leg and she drew her eyes away in a hurry. "I brought you some writing paper, envelopes, and stamps," she said, pulling the items out of a small bag and tucking them in my drawer. She turned to me. "Now, I need the letter you got from your father."

"The one you brought last week?" She nodded. When I retrieved it, she snatched it from my hand with a briskness I knew well. "What's wrong?"

"I have questions." She examined the envelope front and back.

"Don't you remember what the letter says?"

Her head snapped up. "How would I know what it says?"

"Because you opened it before you gave it to me."

She sniffed, apparently insulted. "I don't open other people's mail."

"Someone opened it. The seal was broken."

Her eyes flew to me then down again as she pulled the sheet from the envelope and read it, nodding a time or two. Then she tucked both the note and the envelope into her pocket.

"Mutti, that's mine."

She placed her elbows on her knees and leaned toward me. "I'll destroy it for you," she whispered hoarsely, "so it can't be traced."

"Destroy it? But that letter is mine!"

"Shush." Her eyes darted around the room. "Things have changed. I need to protect..." She stopped. "All of your father's letters have been opened before they're delivered. They're watching his mail. They're suspicious of him."

"Who?"

"This letter," she patted her pocket and continued in that whisper, "and several others refer to the film he's used."

"Of course he uses film. He's a photographer."

"The SS tells me some of his film is unaccounted for."

I gasped. "The SS?" What would they want with my father?

"An SS man came to the bakery." My mother's eyes glistened and she blinked the tears away. "Your father signed out twenty-one rolls and has only sent in twelve for developing. The SS wants to know where the other rolls are."

I couldn't speak.

"I hope they think…" she trailed off again, her gaze far away. Then she seemed to remember I was there. "Film would bring good money on the black market. Maybe they think he's selling the extra."

"Papa wouldn't do that!" My voice was loud and defensive. A couple of the ward's visitors glanced our way, and then returned to their private conversations. I took some deep breaths to slow my racing heart, then leaned closer to Mutti and softened my voice. "He wouldn't steal film."

She nodded and said proudly, "Your father's character is above reproach."

"So what does he say about all this?"

She resumed her whisper. "Since they open his mail, I can't write him about it." She leaned toward me, glancing around a little. "You read my note, right? You're being careful? Staying safe?"

"Of course I'm safe, Mutti. I'm in the hospital." What was safer than inside a hospital?

I sat alone on the porch, flipping through magazines. I lost myself in the beautiful photos – close-ups of movie stars in sparkling dresses, stunning men in tuxedos offering bouquets to leading ladies. A voice pulled me back to reality. "Hi, Sophie. It's been a while."

My heart leapt. There in front of me, grinning and pulling up a chair, was Erich. I placed the magazines aside and stammered a bit. "Erich. It's good to see you." I searched his chocolate eyes, wondering what he saw when he looked at me. But I saw only pleasure reflected there. Despite the polio and my scrawny weakness, he was happy to see me. I relaxed.

He drew a wriggling mass of brown fur from inside his jacket and settled it gently in my lap. "I thought you should officially meet Schatzi."

I stared at the three-legged pup. "Is this…" I didn't know how to finish my thought.

He grinned and nodded. "The pup you and Rennie saw by that shed. I snuck back there a dozen times during the night to put her on the mother's teat. I smuggled her home inside my jacket." He scratched under her dark muzzle. "Hardly even whimpered, she was so weak. Anyway, remember how my Etta had pups just the week before?" I nodded. "She accepted this one and let her nurse."

I cupped my hands around the pup's softness as she burrowed into my lap blanket. "Hey girl. It's good to see you." I looked to Erich. "Wasn't her hind leg…"

He nodded again, his expression serious. "Badly deformed. It had to be amputated. But she's all right now. The vet says she's healthy." He touched a gentle hand to the pup's ear and she nestled her head against his palm.

"Well, little cat. I brought your boyfriend to see you." Klaus pulled up a chair beside Erich.

How embarrassing. I opened my mouth to speak, but Erich lifted his hand to stop me. He spoke first. "Klaus, Sophie's been sick. Please don't make things hard for her." Amazingly, Klaus leaned back, quiet.

Erich faced me again. "So, let's catch up."

"You first."

While I snuggled Schatzi, Erich told stories full of fun about the trip to his grandmother's – how his younger brother let a frog loose in the train's dining car,

81

how his grandfather's parakeet perched on his eyeglasses and moved its head as if reading the newspaper over his shoulder.

Then Klaus chimed in with Youth business. I hadn't spoken with Erich about the book burning or the crucifix incident but with Klaus listening to our every word, this wasn't the time to ask.

I decided to ask for an update. "What about that Youth horsemanship program you applied for, Erich?"

He grinned broadly. "I leave next week."

Erich would be gone too. Everyone was leaving. No one would be around to visit me. I gulped. "How long will you be away?"

He shrugged. "They say between three and six months. First we learn some basics of horse care and riding, then we learn how to train them. I'll be in charge of two or three horses." His eyes brightened as he spoke, his excitement obvious.

"What are the horses being trained for?" Klaus wanted to know.

"Parades, mostly. Maybe some police work in the cities."

I smiled at him. "You'll be good with horses. Look how good you've been with Schatzi."

At her name, the pup's black head lifted and her stubby tail waggled. I handed her over. She nuzzled Erich in complete trust.

Erich kept his face down toward Schatzi, but raised his deep brown eyes and watched me from under his eyebrows. I couldn't get over my good fortune, having Erich the Beautiful visit scrawny weak little me.

Klaus snorted. "Horses. As if we're going to advance the Fatherland with parades and police and old-fashioned cavalry." He glanced at his watch. "We don't have much time. Youth meeting tonight."

Erich sighed. "Ten more minutes."

Klaus excused himself, to use the lav I guess, and I was glad. It gave Erich and me a chance to speak alone. "Sophie, I wanted to tell you about, well, you know..." he hesitated.

I perched my elbows on my thighs, angling close enough to enjoy that distinct earthy scent I knew as Erich. I was almost close enough to touch him. "Tell me what?"

He had trouble starting again, as if he lost his train of thought. I hoped I was the cause of that. He cleared his throat. "I love animals, always have. When I heard about this horse training unit I thought – now there's a way I can be a Youth member and take care of animals too." He shrugged. "Maybe Klaus is right, maybe it is old-fashioned like the cavalry. It's just that..." he trailed off.

He scratched Schatzi under the chin, and the dog's muzzle tipped upward, begging for more. "If I'm with animals, I'll be watching out for them instead of, well, you know. Sometimes when I'm with the other boys, I get carried away and do things..." he glanced at me, then looked at his shoes and shook his head, "things I regret."

I thought of my broken promise to Papa. "I've done things I regret too."

"You?" He seemed surprised. "That's hard to believe. You don't do anything risky. You just run away and hide."

I'd heard it often enough from Klaus but hearing it from Erich was different – his words stung like a thousand bees. I dropped my head.

He stammered. "I'm sorry, Sophie. I didn't mean anything. It's just that, oh…" he stood, cradling Schatzi and pacing.

That's when Klaus returned. "Ah, trouble in paradise I see. Let's go, Erich." He patted my head. "Goodbye little cat. I'll write if you'll write."

Erich shuffled his feet nervously. "Just when I thought I could stop regretting things, I go and say something stupid. I hope you'll forgive me, Sophie." They left without another word.

Part of me wanted to yell at Erich's retreating figure, to tell him how rude it was to speak that way to a sick person, to someone he seems to care about. But another part of me knew that what he said was true.

When I crawled into bed that night, I tugged the blanket up over my head. The dark heavy silence it brought left me with only my own thoughts for company. I barely slept for all the noise.

The next morning before breakfast, I penned a note I didn't intend to send.

*Dear Erich,*

*What you said upset me, but you were right. I do run away and hide when trouble comes. But now I have polio and I can't hide from that.*

*The Youth leaders say that all of us here at the hospital are useless to the Reich because of our weakness, and I'd be useless too if it weren't for my photography skills. But look at Schatzi – she's not useless! She can grow up and live happily as a three-legged dog.*

*You said you're tired of living with regrets. I'm tired of living in hiding. I wish I had the courage to*

I stopped mid-sentence. If I had courage, what exactly would I do? Since I didn't know the answer, I folded the letter and tucked it under my mattress.

## 18 May, Wednesday

Frau Berkheimer watched over my shoulder as Marla and I varnished a wood shelf. "Is your camera in the ward, Sophie?" I nodded. "Go get it."

I was back in no time and showed her which buttons, dials, and levers I needed to work. She looked me square in the eye. "You're ready to do this yourself." Her voice was certain.

My heart raced. "My Papa asked me to take photos of people who help me. I'd like you to be first."

She beamed. "I'd be honored."

I placed the camera on a table and pressed a tiny button to release the bellows. I tugged and gradually the bellows expanded and locked into place. I moved buttons and dials to adjust my settings and even had enough strength to hold the camera while I peered through the viewfinder. I fingered the jagged shutter lever. "Ready?" Click.

I was a real photographer again. We both wiped away tears.

I spent the rest of the week arranging photo shoots of the patients and staff. I jotted down the details – the camera settings, angle, lens used, and lighting. Once I saw the developed shots, I'd learn from my successes and my mistakes. I was back on track with a plan.

# Chapter Seven
## Composition

### 23 May, Monday

Fritz stared at his oatmeal. "What's wrong?" I asked him.

"Every day it's the same thing – eat, wash, and exercise," he said. "Over and over. Nothing fun."

Marla looked up. "We need something to look forward to."

"Like what?" I couldn't imagine anything to look forward to in a hospital, except for visits, letters, and getting discharged of course.

"How about a contest?" Anna said, "Relay races with prizes." Leave it to Anna to come up with a competition.

Herr Franken scowled. "Anna, we're all at different stages of our rehabilitation. It wouldn't be fair to pit a big clumsy adult like me against speedy little Fritz." He tousled the boy's blond head.

Marla brightened. "How about a sing-a-long?"

"Or a talent show." I ventured.

Fritz tipped his head. "What kind of talent?"

"I play the zither," Herr Franken said softly.

"I dance," Elisabeth said, then abruptly closed her eyes. "At least I used to."

I pushed on with the idea. "What about you, Marla?"

"I don't know how to do anything," Marla said, slouching a bit in her wheelchair.

Herr Franken turned to her. "You don't need to perform. There's a lot more to a show than the performances."

"You're good at sewing, Marla," Elisabeth offered.

Herr Franken smiled. "Maybe you could make Elisabeth a costume."

Elisabeth's face brightened. "Or a tiara." Marla didn't look convinced, but Elisabeth squeezed her arm and gave a wide-eyed nod to show her excitement.

Anna pointed to little Fritz and me. "What about you two?" Fritz's lower lip began to quiver.

"You could do sound effects," I told him. "You're good at car and truck noises."

"And trains," he added, cheering a bit.

Anna looked pleased. "That leaves you, Sophie."

"I'll photograph the show. I have my camera now, and some film."

"Great," she said. "I'll notify the staff and set a date. So glad I thought of it."

She never changed.


## 24 May, Tuesday

It was quickly decided that our talent show would be in two-and-a-half weeks, on 11 June. With my father away and in some kind of trouble, I couldn't ask him for photography pointers. So between therapies, I stopped at the hospital library to study magazine photos. I grasped a

88

shelf with one hand and stood to reach a pile of magazines. My balance was a little off which made my arm flail, and I knocked half a dozen magazines to the floor. I groaned at my clumsiness and started to sit so I could clean up my mess when something caught my eye. Tucked at the back of the shelf, now partly exposed by the shortened magazine stack, was a bundle wrapped in brown paper. Curious, I pulled it out and plopped in my wheelchair. A couple dozen photos spilled out.

The photographer had an expensive camera and a keen eye. Some shots were scenic – a hillside covered with wildflowers, a narrow valley dotted with homes, a lone church spire reaching bravely into the sky. There were farm folk with crooked-toothed smiles and dirty hands, panoramic mountain vistas, and close-ups of everyday rural life.

Partway through the pile, farmhouses gave way to townhouses, and storefronts lined bustling streets. One shot showed a crowd cheering and waving as Wehrmacht soldiers marched past.

In the hall, voices drew my attention. Two men. I wasn't doing anything wrong, not really, but I was snooping. Hurriedly, I shaped the bundle of photos to its original size, stood, and tucked it behind the magazines. I had just plopped in my chair when the door opened.

"And then we can…" It was Doktor Vogel. He froze, his hand still on the doorknob while Herr Franken plodded in a few steps behind, one eyebrow raised in an unspoken question.

I smiled my most innocent smile. "Dropped these," I said, picking up the scattered magazines and piling them on my lap. The two men watched me silently until I pushed away.


## 27 May, Friday

Gisela lowered the needle on a gramophone. Tchaikovsky's *Waltz of the Flowers*. "Plié."

Elisabeth swept one arm wide while the other held her crutch, bending her knees about halfway and working hard to maintain her balance.

"Relevé."

Elisabeth's weak right leg, braced below the knee, couldn't rise onto toes, but she managed to rise onto the toes of her left foot. She swept her right arm into a delicate arch while she balanced on one crutch. Her whole body was curved into a C and holding it seemed impossible. But hold it she did, while Gisela counted, "One, two, three, and down." Elisabeth returned to a standing position, right hand curled daintily in front of her hips, left hand trembling on the crutch.

Gisela applauded and I raced over. "That was fantastic!" I told Elisabeth, noting the sweat on her brow.

She collapsed into a chair, obviously pleased and proud. "Not like it was before the polio, but I've still got a few moves."

"Now we have to put those moves together into a dance," Gisela said. "Just two or three minutes long. Want to start tomorrow?"

Elisabeth ran a hand across her forehead then wiped her palm on her skirt. "Give me five minutes rest. Then I'll be ready."

And she was. I admired her.

That afternoon, I pulled out the unfinished letter to Erich and continued where I left off.

*I wish I had the courage to do what my friend Elisabeth is doing. She's going to dance in our talent show, brace and crutch and all. She sure doesn't hide from trouble!*
*Sophie*
*P.S. How is Schatzi? Who's caring for her now that you're gone?*

I mailed it.

A couple letters arrived for me that day. The one from Papa had a broken seal, tiny shreds of paper stuck where the envelope had been opened and poorly re-glued. Papa didn't say if he knew his mail was being opened, and I had no way to warn him.

The second letter disturbed me as much as Papa's.

*Use the film to photograph the talent show.*
*Until the 11th,*
*Scharführer Werner Müller*

# 1 June, Wednesday

Marla guided doe-brown fabric through a sewing machine in OT, creating a small mound at her feet. "What are you making?" I asked.

She lifted her foot from the machine's pedal and looked up, her expression anxious. "Can't you tell?"

I tipped my head to one side to examine the pile from another angle. "A costume of…"

91

She glanced at Frau Berkheimer then looked back at me. "It's the lion," she said, "the lion Hercules meets." A play for the talent show.

"Oh, I see it now." I pointed to the fabric that hung from the machine's needle. "That's a leg."

Marla dropped her hands, letting the cloth puddle on the floor. Frau Berkheimer hurried over and said, "Actually, that's the tail. We're going to stuff it with goose feathers." She nodded at me, urging me to see what she saw.

"Oh, of course," I said trying to smile. "That'll be a great tail." But I pushed to a different workstation in a hurry.

Anna was nearby, directing several patients as they painted the backdrop for Hercules' trip to the Augean stables. "How can we fit three thousand oxen on this one sheet?" Fritz asked her, gesturing to the table-sized piece of paper.

"Make brown dots," Anna said.

Elisabeth grinned at him. "Lots and lots of brown dots."

Anna's lips pressed together. "Now don't let the dots run together. We have to be able to see them individually."

Fritz went to work with his small paintbrush, his voice sing-song. "Ox-dots, ox-dots, lots and lots of ox-dots." Elisabeth giggled.

"What do you want me to do?" I asked Anna.

She gestured to a bolt of fabric and some shears on a nearby table. "Get started on the headpiece for Hydra, the nine-headed monster. The pattern is on top, and pins too."

"I don't know how to sew."

She threw up her hands. "Can't you do anything but sit around and take pictures? If this show is going to be good enough for our guests…" Abruptly, she bustled off somewhere.

Herr Franken shook his head and gestured to me. "What do you say we try this together?" He poked a thumb toward the fabric. "I don't know how to sew either, but I've watched my Gabriele pin patterns and cut them out. How hard can it be?"

He and I worked together for thirty minutes or so, smoothing the fabric and pinning the paper pattern into place. By the time we cut out nine necks and their nine dragon-like heads, we were laughing at our own clumsy efforts.

Fritz and Elisabeth, tired of their ox-dots, came over to inspect. Fritz picked up one of the Hydra-heads as if it were a puppet and thrust it at Elisabeth and me, growling with all the ferocity a six-year-old can muster. We shrieked in mock terror, laughing, as did Frau Berkheimer and a couple other patients.

Only Marla, stuffing the last of the feathers in the lion's tail, wasn't amused. "If Anna sees you do that, she'll be mad."

"Mad about what?" he asked. "About this?" He snuffled and snorted and thrust the fabric head at the lion's tail in Marla's hand. She screamed just as Anna entered the OT room.

"What's wrong?" Anna demanded, bustling over.

Frau Berkheimer smiled. "It's all right, Anna. They're just playing."

"Enough playing," Anna said, ignoring the OT and snatching the Hydra-head from Fritz's hand. I heard the tell-tale rip. Caught beneath Fritz's wheel, the head had torn clean off.

Anna stared at the piece in her hand, then rounded on little Fritz. "Look what you did! You and your horseplay."

Fritz looked from the piece in Anna's hand to the one under his wheel and hung his head. Elisabeth placed her arm around his shoulder and snapped, "You're the one who ripped it, Anna."

Anna glared at Elisabeth then whirled back to the little boy. "Fritz, you need to do your part to move this project forward. If you can't help, then stay out of the way."

Herr Franken walked to the little boy's side and Frau Berkheimer marched over to Anna. "I need to speak with you. Now." She gestured to the door and they left the room.

Several patients murmured kind things to Fritz, about how it wasn't his fault, we were all just having a good time, that sort of thing. Marla sat still and silent until there was a lull in the conversation. Then she said, "I told you she'd be mad," whirled, and pushed out of the room.

Herr Franken shook his head. "You know Fritz, you're just like Hercules." He gave the boy a smile. "You've defeated the Hydra by ripping off her head." Fritz's expression shifted slowly and became a tentative grin.

Then Anna marched back in the room, stooping and snatching the torn costume pieces and clutching them to her chest. She fluttered one hand dramatically. "I'll finish this costume myself." Then she turned on her heel and stomped from the room.

## 4 June, Saturday

My mother's visit was all business. She switched my clean and dirty clothes, smoothed my quilt, pecked me on the head, and left. I hadn't seen Uta and Marie since the first visitation day, hadn't even heard from them by post. And with Klaus, Erich, and Rennie away, I didn't expect any other visitors. Sitting around in the ward room while everyone else enjoyed their company would be depressing, so I decided to take a better look at those scenic photos in the library. Maybe some of the photos in magazines too.

The library smelled of lemon oil polish and the shelves gleamed, slick and dust-free. I stood at the same shelf where I'd stood before, left leg trembling, fingers sliding on the light oily film. But behind the books was nothing – no bundle of photos, nothing but empty space. The cleaning lady must have moved the photos.

I plopped in my chair and made my way down the shelves, standing, sitting, searching, pulling volumes forward and looking behind. Nothing. I scanned the room, frustrated, hoping to spy the stack in some obvious place. In an orderly pile of newspapers and magazines on a bottom shelf, a thick newspaper was turned a bit sideways. I grabbed it.

Somehow, I wasn't surprised to find a stack of photos inside the newspaper. I fanned through them in search of those lovely rural landscapes I'd admired. They weren't there.

Different photos.

The first few showed parading Wehrmacht soldiers, Party flags, and painted signs welcoming the Führer. In one, the smiling Führer accepted flowers from schoolchildren and waved to a cheering crowd. Similar scenes had been in our newspapers and the cinema newsreels for months – the *Anschluss*, the incorporation of Austria back into our Fatherland.

In the next photo, a dozen or so people, adults, children, and Wehrmacht soldiers, stood in a semi-circle. Each face showed a different expression. Some seemed surprised, some pleased. One suited old gentleman appeared stoic, almost blank, while several others looked as if they'd seen a ghost. A young woman covered the eyes of a small child and a meter or two away, a Wehrmacht soldier's head was thrown back in laughter.

In the center of the shot were eight or ten people crouched on all fours, some with faces close to the ground, a couple with heads raised and grass tucked in the sides of their mouths. I tried to imagine the where and why behind the photo. Probably a stunt from *Karnevale* or *Oktoberfest*. I placed it aside and lifted the next photo.

Another crowd of people, some in Wehrmacht uniforms again, standing around a half-dozen men and women who scrubbed a cobblestone street on their hands and knees. Why would soldiers watch festival-goers do stunts?

One of the men had reared up from his position, exposing the breast of his shirt. On it rested a six-pointed star. The man was a Jew. I caught my breath.

The shirts of the other people on the ground were hidden from view. Maybe they were Jews too, maybe not. But a closer look at the hurt, shamed expressions on their faces made it clear – members of the German army were humiliating them in public. And other citizens stood by while it happened, doing nothing.

And that's when it hit me. I was just like them.

When I could have said goodbye to Esther publicly I marched right past, ignoring her pleading eyes. When I saw crucifixes destroyed by bullets, I turned my camera away. When Anna accused Fritz of tearing the fabric, I stayed silent even though I knew she'd done it herself.

If I were home, I'd confess my guilt to the priest, say my Penance, and try to do better. But there were no priests in rehabilitation.

So right there, head pressed against the library table, I whispered, "Dear God, the only way I've ever prayed is by reciting the holy words I've been taught. Papa says that you like it when people just talk to you. It feels disrespectful, but I'll try.

"Father in heaven, Mary Holy Mother, these photos make me feel ashamed, ashamed that when I had the chance, I didn't do what I could. I've been part of a group who pick on other people, who are mean and bossy and cruel. I've seen it happen, and I've done nothing about it. I've stood back silently, blending into the background just like the bystanders in the photos. I'm as guilty as they are. Please forgive me.

"I've done this because I'm afraid. I'm afraid that if I draw attention to myself, something might happen to me the way it happened to Esther and her father.

"Please God, I'm weak and in a wheelchair. Take away my fear of exposure, the fear of standing apart from the crowd. Grant me courage to do what I can so I don't have to feel guilty anymore."

I said a couple of Our Fathers and Hail Marys, then added an Act of Contrition for good measure. I hoped the courage would come soon.

# Chapter Eight
## Lenses

## 6 June, Monday

The wax seal crackled as I opened the envelope.

*Dear Sophie,*

*I'm involved in an important project: building the greatest highway in Europe. We work long hours, but our work is vital. This highway is the cornerstone for the Führer's plan. It will become part of a completely modern network of rails and roads throughout the Fatherland, and I'm part of it.*

*Klaus*

Klaus had thrown all his energy into this new venture, as usual. I wondered how long his enthusiasm would last.

The next envelope had been clumsily resealed.

*My dear Sophiela,*

*We have spent several weeks in beautiful Vienna, where Mozart, Mahler, Brahms, and Beethoven once lived. My heart hears their music even though my ears hear only our tramping boots.*

*When I get grouchy about my blistered feet, I think of you. You are so brave, doing your exercises and getting stronger. I am sure it is hard, painful work. I am most proud of you.*

*Have you taken any photos?*

*Your Papa*

As in every letter from my father, I could almost hear his voice as I read. I longed to hug him, to talk with him. The two months he'd been gone felt like forever.

The last letter in the pile was addressed in familiar looping, rounded script. I smiled as I broke the wax seal.

*Dear Sophie,*

*I've settled in with the other girls from BDM in a town called Freising about thirty kilometers from Munich. I help the farmer's wife with housework and her four small children. I love it, making jam with her and caring for the little ones.*

*Uta and Marie are on this same farm, but they've been assigned to work with the animals, feeding, watering, and cleaning stalls. I only see them once or twice a week because they live in the bunks and I live in the main house. Uta seems annoyed by the hard messy work and I think she's jealous that I'm at the house. What she doesn't understand is that being the only teenager at the house gets lonely sometimes.*

*Write me soon! I miss you.*

*Your friend always,*

*Rennie*

I smiled at the thought of Rennie rolling out pie dough while a toddler played with blocks at her feet. Marie was strong and probably enjoyed the physical work of the farm. But I couldn't picture Uta there at all. How would she cope, mucking a stall, her shapely curves hidden by coveralls, her trim fingernails buried under coarse work gloves, and her long, silky hair pulled back tight while she shoveled dung and hoisted buckets of feed?

Maybe I ought to write to Marie and Uta and tell them about… about what? My daily struggles to exercise and try to walk? The disturbing photos? The upcoming talent show?

They'd react the same way they had during visitation. They'd fidget and be quick to push the letter aside.

They probably didn't want to be friends with me anymore, now that I was crippled. I didn't want them to feel obligated to write me, to feel sorry for me. My chin trembled. If they still wanted to be my friends, they'd have to write first.

I settled back to write responses to people who truly cared about me, whether I was crippled or not.

*Dear Papa,*

*I don't feel brave, stuck here doing my exercises. I'm afraid of so many things.*

I stopped a moment. Someone in the Party would probably read this letter. Should I cross that out? Would they assume I was doing something to make me afraid? Then I remembered my prayer, took a deep breath, and forged on.

*I've asked God for courage.*

*I've taken a few photos of the staff and patients here, but I'm saving most of my film for our big talent show this Saturday. I'm the official photographer!*

*I'll write next week and tell you all about it. I wish I could tell you in person.*

*Your Sophiela*

I reread it, still second-guessing myself in case someone intercepted the letter between the hospital and Papa. But eventually, I did send it as is. Maybe that showed some of the courage I'd prayed for but it didn't feel very divine.

*Dear Rennie,*

*What a wonderful way to spend a work summer! Those children are lucky to have you as a mother's helper.*

*Everyone here is excited about the upcoming talent show. Anna has put herself in charge — no surprise there. The Pied Piper will take my film for developing afterward. I'll show you the photos when I see you in November.*

*Your friend always,*
*Sophie*

## 10 June, Friday

Dress rehearsal was to start right after our midday meal. Anna strode around the chaos in the ward, clipboard and pen in hand, barking orders to move people and props. Frau Berkheimer helped little ones into costumes. Gisela arranged crutches and walkers for patients who would perform while standing.

I was figuring out where to position myself for the best shots when a small voice came behind me. "Chugga, chugga, choo-choo!" It was Fritz, his scrawny arms pushing his wheelchair as he dragged a basket holding the day's mail. "Make way for the train!" He slowed a bit. "There's one in there for you, Sophie," he said, before taking off again. I retrieved the letter as he chugged off.

The return address was unfamiliar but I recognized the handwriting. I hurried out onto the porch so I could read Erich's letter alone.

*Dear Sophie,*

*I'm glad you're not angry with me. My mother says I need to place a guard at my mouth, and I think she's right.*

*I'm at the horse farm and between grooming, cleaning the stables, learning to ride, and training the horses, I work seven days a week from sun up until sun down. It's late at night now, but I wanted to write before another day slips away. No more regrets, remember?*

*I left my little brother Karl in charge of Schatzi while I'm gone. He tells me she plays well with the other dogs and has a special fondness for chewing shoes. Maybe I'll need to visit the shoemaker when I get home!*

*Your letter made me smile. Write again soon.*
*Erich*

The screen door banged open and a head popped around the frame. Anna, looking agitated. "There you are. I'm always rounding up stragglers. Aren't you supposed to watch the dress rehearsal so you could plan your shots?"

"Coming right now." I tucked Erich's letter into my blouse pocket, close to my heart.

There were a dozen acts in the show including the long Hercules play with its props, backdrops, and costumes. Fritz's monster sound effects added great fun to the serious tale, especially the scene with Hydra. I arranged myself on the right side of the actors, stage left Anna called it, to get the best view of the many scenes and backdrops. When singers or musicians performed, center stage was a better position. I jotted down my plans – where I'd position myself, which lens I'd use, which settings. That would minimize mistakes during the actual show.

Marla pulled up beside me. "Did you see Elisabeth's tiara?"

I craned my neck and saw Elisabeth waiting, applauding the others' performances. She looked every bit the ballerina as she sat there, her straight back and long neck, made longer by her coiled bun. Her bun was topped by a shiny silver something. "Where did it come from?"

Her smile told the answer. "I made it out of a head band and some tin foil."

"Very clever." I meant it. "It looks great."

Marla glanced over at her creation then back at me. "You don't suppose it'll fall off if she does one of those spinning moves that ballerinas do?"

I patted her hand. "It'll be fine." Honestly, losing the tiara was the least of the embarrassing things that could happen to Elisabeth. Of all the participants in the show, her performance was the riskiest. The dance's physical exertion and delicate balance left her exposed to ridicule and possible humiliation. With all my heart, I wanted her to succeed. So did Gisela, judging by the way she hovered near the gramophone, wiping her hands against her skirt and glancing repeatedly at Elisabeth.

I noticed something I'd missed before. Elisabeth's hands were trembling.

When it was her turn, she stood, adjusted the crutch's clamp around her left forearm, and waddled to center stage. She took a few deep breaths then posed, framed by the ward's large windows, her pale pink tulle skirt settling around her thin hips. Below the skirt was one shapely leg and dainty pink pointe shoe; beside it, one scrawny leg encircled by a below-the-knee brace, clamped with metal stirrups to a brown orthopedic shoe. Gisela nodded at her and dropped the needle.

I reminded myself of my own job – to find the correct angles and lighting to photograph the dance. I moved from one side of the room to the other during the first minute or two, finally settling on stage left. I jotted down my position and camera settings to best capture her action shots.

Once she was dancing, Elisabeth seemed at ease, moving one arm gracefully while the other grasped the supporting crutch. She used the crutch as a pivot, dancing in circles around it a few times, shifting her weight hard but balancing, always balancing. As her finale, while one foot was earthbound by leather and metal, the other rose into the air courtesy of that elegant pink shoe. She posed there, right arm raised delicately overhead.

She was amazing.

When Gisela lifted the needle Elisabeth bowed, smiling. All of us patients hooted and whistled and applauded. Her buddy Fritz clapped so hard his face grew red and his cheeks threatened to burst. Gisela rushed her, sweeping her into a hug and spinning her in a circle, the crutch flying high. Frau Berkheimer and Doktor Vogel offered their congratulations, wiping their eyes.

And then there was Anna. When I'd have expected her to be bursting with pride at such an accomplishment, she jotted notes on her clipboard, clapped her hands twice, and called for silence. "Lots of things need to be fixed if you're going to be ready to be seen by," she hesitated, "by your loved ones." Everyone groaned. She glanced around, her expression annoyed. "What if the Führer came to this show?"

From somewhere to the left of me I heard a mumbled, "Did you send him a telegram?" Several people gasped. There stood Elisabeth, tiara askew, sweat on her brow, staring at Anna with an expression of defiance and triumph. Anna raised one eyebrow, regarded her, and then stormed from the room.

## 11 June, Saturday

The excitement was unmistakable. Beds and furniture were pushed to the rear to create a large open area in front of the ward windows. Everyone chattered and fussed with hair and fingernails and glanced anxiously at the clock.

Anna marched into the crowded ward and clapped her hands. "Attention, please. Attention. Our talent show will begin in thirty minutes. Performers, go to the OT room for costumes. Guests, please find a seat." She gestured to rows of folding chairs.

Herr Franken stopped in front of Mutti and me. "Frau Adler, Sophie, can you come help with costumes?"

My mother had been fidgety during the awkward pre-show time, and she seemed glad for some task. So she followed the performers and me to the OT room where she helped as needed, smiling and offering kind words, adjusting straps and barrettes and headpieces. The tender Mutti was back. When the show started, she settled in one of the folding chairs and gave me a supportive nod.

Most of the acts went as rehearsed including Herr Franken's zither and a folk singer's solo. Click. Click.

When the woman who fancied herself an opera singer took the stage, I stifled a giggle. Same for the tuba player. Click. Click.

I shot the various scenes of the Hercules play with its different actors and backdrops and costume changes. Judging by the murmurs of approval and rounds of giggles and applause, Fritz's sound effects and Marla's costumes were well received. Both of them beamed. Click. Click.

I turned to Anna a couple times during the play. Her lips were pressed as tight as the papers in her clipboard and she glanced out the windows often. Click.

As the Hercules backdrops were taken down and the little table for the Cat's Cradle girls was set up Anna finally smiled, her eyes following something or someone into the building. I couldn't see what or who she saw until he entered the ward and saluted.

Werner. I'd forgotten he was coming today.

Anna echoed his salute and she kept her eyes fixed on him. The room hushed, then chairs scraped the floor as a number of guests and patients rose and repeated the salute. Marla did, and little Fritz, but not Elisabeth, not Herr Franken nor his wife Gabriele, and to my surprise, not my mother.

Mutti sat in that folding chair, staring straight ahead with her lips moving silently and hands stuffed in skirt pockets. She was several meters away from me, too far for me to see small details. I turned my camera toward her and zoomed in on a pocket. Her knuckles, bumping against the cloth, showed slow rhythmic movement and intermittent readjustment.

My mother was saying her rosary instead of saluting. Click.

Later that night, I wrote:

*Dear Rennie,*

*Our talent show had a dozen acts and everyone enjoyed performing for their relatives and friends. After each act, Anna found some excuse to step onstage, even if was just in a corner. Then she'd bow along with the contestant during the applause. She hasn't changed a bit.*

*My favorite act, Elisabeth doing ballet, went well. She even tried a pirouette! She's being discharged on Monday. I'm going to miss her.*

*I hope my photos come out all right, especially the action shots of Elisabeth's dance. Werner will bring me the prints in a couple weeks. And he gave me two fresh rolls of film!*

*Write soon.*

*Your friend,*

*Sophie*

# Chapter Nine
## Prints

## 18 June, Saturday

After the chaos leading up to the talent show, the following week was a welcome relief. My mother sent a letter by post saying she was ill and wouldn't visit so I had a full day ahead with no visitors, no therapy, and nothing to plan. I headed to the porch to read and catch up on my letters, maybe play a little solitaire in peace and quiet.

I'd just settled in with a few magazines when heavy footsteps drew my attention. Werner. "I, I didn't know you were coming today," I said.

He pulled an envelope from an inside pocket and tossed it in my lap. His way of giving me something without getting too close. "Your photos."

"From the show? They're done already?" I was surprised.

He nodded crisply. I lifted the envelope – it felt light, quite a bit lighter than I expected. "Is this all that came out? From two rolls of film?"

"These are the photos you may keep. The rest of the photos are," one corner of his mouth formed a strange smile, "useless to you."

My stomach twisted at that word. But this was my chance to be courageous, to tell him what I needed. I took a deep breath. "You should have brought the other prints anyway. That's how I learn. I note my settings and then decide how the lighting and shutter speed affected the..." He turned and left before I finished my sentence.

Does speaking up count as courage if no one listens?

I opened the envelope and slid out the prints. Only twenty-two, less than half of what I'd photographed. A few at the top I'd forgotten about, ones I'd taken weeks before. One of Elisabeth and Fritz racing in the hallway showed Fritz's eyes scrunched shut and Elisabeth's mouth twisted in a grimace. Like many of my action shots, I'd captured the wrong moment. I threw that print in the trash.

But my still shots – Marla and her ringlets as she stood in the parallel bars, Anna, content as a student nurse before she tried to turn the ward into a new version of her Youth troop – they came out well.

I shuffled to the photos of the talent show. Again, I was pleased with the way I'd captured the essence of each performance and the participants, although admittedly I caught them all in static poses. I searched the stack for the action shots of Elisabeth's dance. They weren't there. I'd taken six or eight of the dance alone. How could all of them be gone?

I started again at the top of the stack and noticed something else. The shot of Mutti's pocket full of rosary beads was missing also.

My gut registered fear.

## 23 June, Thursday

A letter in Papa's handwriting waited on my bed. Again, the envelope had been opened and poorly resealed.

*My dear Sophiela,*

   *I hope you are taking photos. Tell the truth. Be careful.*
   *I will always be,*
   *Your loving Papa*

Nothing else. Something was wrong. I needed to talk to my mother, to find out if she'd heard from him. I needed to use the telephone. The only one I knew of was in Doktor Vogel's office. Surely he'd give me permission to use it. He and Papa were old friends.

I pushed to the doctor's office and knocked. No answer. I tried the doorknob. Locked. Probably gone for the day. A phone call was out until morning. I'd have to wait at least twelve hours.

I had to do something to pass the time, something to take my mind off that letter. A new book. That's what I needed.

I poked among the volumes in the library, tipping my head to read the sideways titles. I settled on a newspaper from the pile on the bottom shelf. Maybe I could catch up with what was happening at the cinema, in Altstadt, and… I slid it out of the stack and tucked it next to my hip.

The one below it grabbed my attention. There, on the crumpled front page, was a familiar photo. People scrubbing the streets. The exact same photo I'd held in my own hands a couple weeks before, right in that same library. I snatched it up and read the newspaper's banner – London. With both papers at my hip, I pushed to my usual private spot on the end of the porch.

I unfolded the German paper first, *Völkischer Beobachter*. "The Party's version of a newspaper," my father always called it. For some reason, I noticed the subtitle beneath the paper's title banner, maybe for the first time. *Kampfblatt der national-sozialistischen Bewegung Grossdeutschlands.* Military Journal of the National Socialist Movement of Greater Germany.

Military journal? I shuddered and tossed the newspaper aside.

I pulled out the paper from London dated a few days earlier. No doubt about it; that front page photo was the one I'd seen in the library. I scanned the caption and the accompanying article alongside it, hoping to recognize some of the English words. The only ones I understood were proper names – Vienna, Salzburg, Reich, Austria, and Jew. "Jew" was written at least a dozen times, twice in the caption alone. At the end of the article were some words and the number 6 in parentheses.

I flipped to page six and spread the paper across the width of my wheelchair. I caught my breath. In front of me was another familiar photo – people with mouthfuls of grass. I scanned the caption. The words Austria and Jew again. I could barely think straight. In. Out. In. Out.

Someone passed those two photos through the hospital, my hospital, right through my very hands before sending them to a London newspaper. That someone wanted the people of England to know about the plight of Austrian Jews. If that someone was

German, he or she might be accused of betraying the Fatherland.

Treason.

The Party would find out who took the photos and who sent them. That person or persons would be held accountable.

My mind wouldn't settle that night, spinning and making connections. A courageous person, an insider, had taken photos that showed the Reich's wrongdoing. My gut told me it might be Papa. Even knowing the risk, he would have done it. The thought filled me with pride. And with terror.

I needed to know what my mother knew.

## 24 June, Friday

Before breakfast, I went to see Doktor Vogel. He looked up from the papers strewn across his desk and smiled. "You're up and around early, Sophie. What can I do for you?"

"I need to use the telephone."

He tilted his head. "Is there a problem?"

"I need to speak with my mother."

He regarded me for a moment and then gestured to the telephone at the edge of his desk. I hoped he'd leave the office so I could speak in private, but he lowered his head to his paperwork. I lifted the receiver and dialed.

When I heard my mother's strong, firm voice, I felt mine quaver. "Hello, Mutti. It's me, Sophie."

"*Ja*, Sophie." Her volume rose in concern. "*Was ist los?* What's the matter?"

I took a breath and glanced at Doktor Vogel. Engrossed in his paperwork. I forged on and whispered into the phone. "Have you heard from Papa?"

The doctor peered at me over his spectacles.

"I got a letter last Tuesday."

I turned away from the watching doctor and spoke directly into the receiver. "Well, the one I got yesterday frightened me."

My mother's usual husky pitch rose to that of an adolescent girl. "We cannot speak of this on the phone. I'll visit tomorrow." There was a click and the line went dead. Stunned, I dropped the receiver on the hook.

Doktor Vogel's intense blue eyes regarded me and slowly, deliberately, he lowered his pen. "Tell me what's happened." His voice was smooth as velvet over the jagged edges of my breath. "If there's something I could do to help…" He left his offer unfinished.

I wanted to trust him. He'd been friends with Papa since they were boys. He'd been our family's doctor for as long as I could remember. I just couldn't find my voice.

He continued softly. "I stopped by the library this morning to read a newspaper or two but they weren't where I left them." Heat rose into my cheeks. "I saw them on your nightstand when I did rounds. You're welcome to them. Just return them later."

I stared silently at my shoes, chiding myself for leaving the newspapers in plain sight.

He leaned toward me. "Can you read English?"

I shook my head but kept my eyes down. Gently, his finger lifted my chin so I had to meet his gaze. What I saw was the familiar soft, kind expression he always wore. So like Papa. No wonder they were friends.

"Sophie Adler, I've known your family since before you were born. I'd never harm you. Do you believe that?"

When I remained silent, he sighed. "I see." He took off his spectacles and wiped them with a pocket handkerchief. "You'll have to pardon me, but I overheard your conversation. I assume your father's letter alluded to something dangerous but gave no specifics. Is that right?"

I nodded.

"Perhaps the time has come." From his vest pocket, he pulled out a tiny key and used it to unlock a desk drawer. He shuffled through a stack of papers, isolated a single envelope, and handed it to me.

I started to ask, "What…" but he gestured with his chin. I flipped the envelope and saw the red wax seal pressed with my Adler family crest.

I slid my finger beneath the seal and lifted. The wax crackled. Doktor Vogel had not opened this letter.

I really could trust him.

*My dearest Sophiela,*

*If you are reading this letter, the situation must be critical. Try to be brave.*

*I have used my camera to capture the full story of the Reich. Others have risked much to spread that story to the rest of the world. I cannot tell you more now, but I hope someday I can.*

*I could do nothing but follow my heart and show the whole truth. If you do the same, I will always be proud of you.*

*Your loving Papa*

I reread the letter several times and my vision blurred. Doktor Vogel watched as I blew my nose, his eyebrows furrowed into a single crease, his little pyramid of fingertips tapping rhythmically, expectantly.

Swallowing my fear I folded the letter, slid it in the envelope, and tucked it in my pocket. If Doktor Vogel was disappointed that I didn't show it to him, he didn't let on. "My father says he's been taking photographs," I reported, my voice weaker than I'd have liked, "and that I should follow my heart."

"Sound advice." He rose and walked to the door, opened it a crack, peered out, closed it, and turned the key.

I straightened and waited, my heart pounding.

"Your father's a talented photographer," he began in a low whisper once he sat again. "He's been traveling with the Wehrmacht to photograph their," he hesitated as if searching for a good word, "their adventures. Your father is also a man of conscience." He leaned forward and perched his forearms on the desk, again tapping those fingertips. "What your father saw, he photographed. Soon he realized he was photographing things the Reich wouldn't want the outside world to see."

"How do you know?"

He hesitated a moment then pushed on. "He couldn't send the rolls containing those photos to the Wehrmacht film developer. Nor could he destroy them. His conscience wouldn't allow it. So he sent the rolls of film and instructions on handling them," he hesitated another moment, before finishing, "to a trusted friend."

I was barely aware of my whispered response. "You."

Doktor Vogel nodded. "I took them to the developer in Schwabing that your father always used. I paid that man handsomely to keep silent about the content of the photos, and God bless him, he didn't ask questions. Because I've refused to join the Party I have, shall we say, a reputation with them, so I couldn't keep the prints at my home." He sighed and continued. "I hid the prints in an unlikely place, somewhere I had frequent easy access, but also somewhere the SS wasn't liable to go."

"Here. In the hospital library."

Out in the corridor, footfalls approached, thudding rhythmically. Unconsciously, my spine stiffened to a rod. The thuds grew louder and then faded. My breath whooshed out.

Doktor Vogel shook his head as if awakening from a dream. He regarded me somberly. "I suggest you destroy the letter I gave you. The one your father sent you by post also." He lifted his pen and bent over his papers. It was clear. I was dismissed.

I took both of Papa's letters out of their envelopes and reread them a couple times, committing the words to memory. I held them over the toilet and flushed, planning to watch them go down the drain. And yet the letters were bits of my father. If I destroyed them and something happened to him...

I folded the letters, stuffed them in their envelopes, and tucked them in my pocket. I'd find some place to hide them. I was good at hiding things. Apparently Papa was too.

117

## 25 June, Saturday

I sat on the porch engrossed in a book when Herr Franken and his wife Gabriele approached. They spun chairs so they could sit facing me. They weren't smiling.

Gabriele handed me a poster twice as long as notebook paper. "Have you seen this?"

The headline for the top half of the poster read, "Should Germany's future look like this?" Below these words, an enlarged photo showed a familiar scene — Klaus, Erich, and the boys from their HJ troop in uniform, holding guns pointed at unseen targets. Targets I knew to be crucifixes.

I'd taken that photo. No doubt this was one of my missing prints. My throat tightened.

The bottom half of the poster was labeled, "Or like this?" Below those words was another of my missing prints, this one an action shot taken at the talent show. It captured a costumed Elisabeth in the middle of her lopsided relevé, her trunk lurched to an impossible angle while her crutch reached for the ground. With her eyes half-shut, her mouth twisted in a grimace, and her tin foil tiara askew, she looked ridiculous.

Elisabeth looked like a freak, a crooked face on top of a grotesquely lopsided body. It was just the kind of unflattering action photo I was afraid I'd take. I'd hoped to throw shots like that in the trash before anyone else could see them. But there, on that poster, that photo lived.

Werner had given my photos to the Party. The Party turned them into this propaganda, their way of telling everyone what to think. That the ordered discipline of the perfect Youth was valuable; the struggling, imperfect Elisabeth was not.

My photos had been used against my friend Elisabeth. Against someone just like me.

In. Out. In. Out.

This poster was my fault. I should have known Werner would hand over my photos. Elisabeth would never forgive me. I would never forgive myself.

"Where did you find this?" My voice was barely audible.

"Tacked to a pole, right near the Marienplatz. For all I know, copies might be all over Munich." Gabriele regarded me. "You took that photo of Elisabeth, didn't you Sophie?"

My voice was a hoarse whisper. "Yes."

"And the other one, the one of the Youth?" I nodded. Herr Franken narrowed his eyes. "Sophie, we don't think you gave permission to use the photos in this way. But others here may not be so understanding."

I looked from one face to the other, trying to understand. No one at the hospital would think I'd approve of this. Would they?


"I have some news," my mother said on arriving for visitation, twisting her hands with palms pressed together. "Your Papa has been detained."

My heart thudded against my ribs. "Detained? What does that mean?"

"He's being questioned."

"Why?" But I already knew the answer. "Because of the photos. Because they were sent to England and published. Because they show the Reich in a bad light."

She regarded me, her eyes narrowed. "What do you know of such things?"

I handed her the cryptic letter Papa sent me by post. "This is the note I called you about."

She read it, made a "Hmpf" sound, and thrust it back to me. "I'll ask you again. What do you know?"

"I saw some photos here at the hospital."

She continued to regard me as if trying to read the rest of the story in my face. "And Herr Doktor Vogel told you that your father was the photographer?"

"Not exactly."

She smacked her hand against her thigh and stood, paced briefly and without another word, marched inside. I pushed after her, but she had a head start.

A dozen meters from Doktor Vogel's office, I heard her raised voice but couldn't make out the words. I hurried closer and pressed my ear against the door.

"… in the middle of your plan!"

Doktor Vogel's soft reply was barely audible but gentle and steady as ever, even in the face of his friend's irate wife. "I'm sorry to upset you so, Karla. Hans is aware of what he has done. I gave the most incriminating photos…" Here he stopped short before continuing. "Suffice it to say this person has connections with a newspaper in London. The rest of the photos, the ordinary ones of scenery and the daily life of the soldiers, had to be returned to Hans."

"And I did my part," my mother interrupted, "sending those back to him in my packages of food and clothing. But England, Alphonse? What if…" Her voice choked on these last words.

The opened letters. Mutti being followed. The SS visit to the bakery. Her abrupt manner on the phone. Finally, it all made sense. I wouldn't have pegged my mother as one to get involved in a scheme like this, but I was proud of her. She had courage.

Rapid footsteps approached and the door swung open. Doktor Vogel glowered at me. "I'm not fond of eavesdroppers. Come in. I want to speak with you anyway."

Inside the office, my mother paced, her fists bulging in her dress pockets and gray hair poking out of her bun like bits of wire.

"Sophie," Doktor Vogel began, "I doubt you knew how your photos would be used." He held the poster – Herr Franken certainly brought it to him quickly.

"What's that?" my mother asked, and he handed it to her without comment. She examined it. "There's my Klaus. The future of Germany. So handsome." I watched her eyes drop to the bottom of the poster and a puzzled look crossed her face. "I know this girl. What's wrong with her?"

"That's Elisabeth." The words stuck in my throat. "She was a patient here."

Slowly, recognition crossed my mother's face. "Elisabeth. The ballerina." She folded her hands around the edges of the poster, then lifted her head abruptly. A spark crossed her face; a new connection had been made. "*Ach, mein Gott!*" She bolted to her feet and glanced from the poster to me and back again. "They're saying that children like this Elisabeth and my Sophie are not…"

Doktor Vogel finished the statement for her. "Not good for Germany's future. Because they are crippled. *Ja.*

121

Useless eaters, they say." He shook his head. "I expect these posters are all around the city, maybe all around the Fatherland." He removed his spectacles, rubbing his eyes before putting them back on and turning to Mutti. "That's why Hans and I felt so strongly. The Party is targeting ... people who are crippled are next."

Car doors slammed and I jumped. Doktor Vogel moved to the window and peered out, leaning a hand against the windowsill. He exhaled in a long sigh, slumping ever so slightly. Then he turned to us, squared his shoulders, and tugged the bottom of his vest into place. "I have visitors. Karla, Sophie, please go. Quickly."

My mother stared past him out the window, her arms limp. The poster slid from her hands.

My heart pounded. "Who's out there?"

Doktor Vogel gestured toward the door. "Best if you aren't seen with me." His tone was still calm even though his manner was urgent. "Please go." He picked up the poster and handed it to me. I didn't want it, but something in his expression made me take it. I stuffed the poster behind my back.

My mother spun and I followed. We didn't get too far. Three SS men in knee-length black coats stood in front of us, a solid inky wall. One sneered, "Going somewhere, ladies?"

# Chapter Ten
## Foreground

My mother's answer was high and breathy. "I'm taking my daughter to the ward." She stepped behind my chair and pushed as if the men would part like the Red Sea before Moses. They didn't. She stopped short, my footrests just shy of their shins.

One of the men moved toward Doktor Vogel and spoke, but the pounding in my ears kept me from hearing his words. He shoved the doctor's shoulder and ushered him past us out of the office and through an exterior door. A black sedan waited there, its back door open like a hungry mouth.

A second man spoke to Mutti and me but I couldn't focus on his words either, just on that gaping car door.

A small knot of people had formed in the hall. Some patients were there with their guests, including my friends Herr Franken and Marla. Anna leaned against a wall, arms crossed on her stomach.

Why was Anna here on her day off?

Another black sedan pulled up behind the first and a fourth uniformed figure marched into the building. Werner. He glanced briefly at the little audience in the hall and exchanged nods with Anna. His high, nasal whine broke through the noise in my ears. "Young Adler should remain here. She's proven quite valuable to the Reich." Werner waved at my mother. "But take the woman." One of the SS men grabbed Mutti's elbow and guided her out. As the open car swallowed her, she glanced briefly at me, her face flush with panic. An SS man climbed in beside her. In moments, the other two SS were in the front seat and the car sped off.

Without another word, Werner saluted and took off after them in the second car.

In the knot of bystanders, a growling voice spoke. Anna, red-faced, pointed an accusing finger at me. "First Elisabeth's photo is posted all around Munich, as if she's some kind of, well, less than human." Had she seen the poster too? "And the photographer? Sophie Adler."

My head spun but no words settled to my lips.

"Now our own Medical Director is taken away by the SS right before our eyes," Anna continued. "And who's in the thick of things? Sophie. And when her own mother is led away, who's left behind?" She clucked her tongue and her eyes flitted from face to face in the group, obviously looking for agreement. "That's right. Sophie."

In. Out. In. Out.

Still she went on. "What did Werner, I mean the Scharführer say? 'She has proven quite valuable to the Reich.'" Anna widened her stance and shoved her fists against her hips, daring anyone to contradict her.

"No!" I tried to protest, but the word was lost in the chaos that erupted in the hallway. Several people shouted and someone screamed.

I raced out of there to the ward and then out onto the porch where I stayed for hours, silent and alone, shivering and weeping. All evening, normal sounds came from indoors, voices, doors closing, music playing, even some laughter. I stayed there long after the sun went down and the cool night air sat damp on my skin. No one came to find me. Obviously, no one cared.

When the ward was finally dark and quiet, I snuck inside, washed and changed and crawled into bed. But not before tucking the poster under my mattress.

No one saw me. It was better that way.


## 26 June, Sunday

I spent most of the day alone on the porch, playing solitaire and pretending to read, but I couldn't concentrate. So many things needed to be sorted out. A talk with an old friend would help.

I hesitated, pen against paper, struggling to find focus for my blurry thoughts and feelings. Eventually, I scribbled

*Dear Rennie,*

*The Pied Piper has used his flute. Rats have attacked me and people I love. I don't know what to do.*

*Sophie*

I reread it a couple times to make sure nothing there would get either of us in trouble. Then I addressed it and started toward the hospital's mail slot.

On my way through the ward, four patients huddled near the radio turned and scowled. They probably believed gossip and rumors told about me. I felt sick.

I wanted to leave, to go far away where no one knew me, where no one knew my family, where there was no polio and no SS and no parents or old family friends in trouble. I pushed faster, dropped my letter to Rennie in the mail slot, and sped down the hall.

I opened the library door and clicked on a table lamp. A beam of yellowed light shot above and below the lampshade and left much of the room's contents in shadow – the shelves filled with dusty volumes and wrinkled newspapers, the half-dozen wooden chairs around the long, empty table, pocked and dinged from years of use. What if more of my father's photos were here, photos Doktor Vogel didn't have time to send to England? What if the SS found me in that room? The back of my neck prickled. I left in a hurry.

That placed me in the darkened, quiet hall in front of the physio room. On weekdays, that area was the hub of activity but here on the weekend, it was still as a tomb. Thin stripes of sunlight pushed between nearly-closed Venetian blinds and warmed the mat tables, the parallel bars, and the floor. I pushed in, transferred onto a mat and closed my eyes.

When I sat up, the stripes had moved up the wall and lost their warmth. Wetness and slime covered my hands, one side of my face, and the mat table. I dried them with my sleeve.

I'd missed supper. I transferred to my wheelchair and pushed past the ward, avoiding all manner of gazes and whispers. Once outside, I retreated to my refuge at the far end of the porch where I hoped to stay, hidden and unnoticed.

## 29 June, Wednesday

No one, not even the staff, really knew what to say to me. When Herr Franken spoke kindly to me, I burst into tears. When little Fritz tried to cheer me with silly sound effects, I forced a quavering smile but stayed quiet. After a couple days, they left me alone to brood.

I was quietly and obediently exercising on a mat in physio when three men bustled in. One, a middle-aged man in a dark blue suit with graying hair combed over a bald spot, twiddled a silvery end of his waxed mustache. Beside him, a uniformed Party officer glared around the room, feet spread and hands behind his back. The third wore the black coat of the SS. His eyes scanned the room and when they fell on me, he raised an eyebrow. I caught my breath. He was one of the men who arrested Mutti and Doktor Vogel. And he recognized me. There I was, lying on a mat in plain sight.

In. Out. In. Out.

"*Heil, Hitler.*" The Party officer snapped his heels and saluted the room full of patients and staff. Several people responded in kind. Gisela, busy with a patient in the parallel bars, stared silently. I propped on my elbows to watch. The officer cleared his throat and continued. "Your new Medical Director, Herr Doktor Georg Albrecht."

The man with the waxed mustache stepped forward and saluted. "I'm in charge here now." His voice boomed through the large room. "The previous Medical Director participated in activities," he paused, "which were ill-advised. Today begins a new era at this hospital. As soon as possible, each of you will be returned to your rightful place in the Reich."

What exactly was the rightful place for me or any of us with our crippled bodies, all of us 'useless eaters'?

The new Medical Director strolled around the physio room, greeting everyone with a general disinterested nod, squeezing and pulling that mustache. He approached my mat table and I hoped he'd nod and pass me by, too. Instead, he stopped beside me and waited while I sat up and arranged my legs over the side of the mat. I reached out my hand as I'd been taught. "Sophie Adler," I said.

He grasped my hand with both of his and pumped it a few times, the pointy mustache ends jiggling as he spoke. "Ah, I've heard much of your talents. I have something for you." He patted his pockets and pulled out a folded paper. A telegram.

I'm pretty sure I stopped breathing. Telegrams meant bad news.

**Received word Mutti also detained. Release from RLS 13 July to work bakery.**
**Klaus**

It was bad news, all right. My stepbrother was coming home.

# 1 July, Friday

I was barely out of bed when Anna came into the ward. "You're needed at the Medical Director's office. Come."

I didn't know what to think of Anna anymore, but I knew I didn't trust her. Yet here I was, and there she was. What else could I do? I followed her.

She rapped on Doktor Albrecht's office door while pushing it open. "She's here, *Vater*."

*Vater*? The new Medical Director was Anna's father?

The man looked up from his desk. *"Danke."* He gestured me closer. Anna closed the door behind her and leaned against it. She was staying for this conversation. Doktor Albrecht sat back in his chair and began to tug his mustache, a habit I found annoying. "I've received word," he said.

My heart jumped. "About what?"

"Your father and the former Medical Director have been formally charged. Treason."

I caught my breath. "Treason," I repeated.

*"Ja,* among other things. They were involved in a plot against the Fatherland."

I could barely muster a whisper. "What, what's the penalty for treason?" I chanced a glance at Anna. She still leaned against the door, a strange expression on her face. Satisfaction?

The doctor didn't answer. "The trial begins September first." He leaned forward to prop his elbows on the desk. "Now at the trial, certain things might be taken into account." My heart hammered so loudly I thought I might miss his words. "Certain favors might be repaid."

"Favors? What kind of favors?"

"Your photographs."

"My photos might get Papa and Doktor Vogel, um," I didn't know how to finish my question.

He stood abruptly. "I can't make deals."

"And my mother?"

"I've told you what I could. *Heil Hitler.*" He saluted and waited for me to do the same. Anna stood near the door, her arm raised in a salute. I ducked under it and left.


## 2 July, Saturday

The treason charge meant my parents and Doktor Vogel were enemies of the Party. Anyone caught helping them would be arrested and charged as well. Even me. My shoulders tightened.

Klaus would be back in Munich in less than two weeks. No doubt he was still excited about the Party's big projects and ideas. The most I could expect from him was neutrality. I wouldn't put it past him to side with the Party, even against Mutti and Papa and the doctor.

Heavy footsteps drew my gaze. "Werner."

He saluted. "You have film for me?"

"Um, no," I stammered. "I, I haven't taken any photos at all. Not since…"

"Keep it that way."

"Excuse me?"

"Don't use the two tins I gave you. Another assignment will come to you shortly." He saluted and was gone.

The whole thing gave me a headache. I put my head down on the porch rail. I must have fallen asleep because a voice startled me. "I thought I might find you out here."

"Rennie!" There she was, right in front of me, hugging me, clasping my hand. "What are you doing here?" I wiped my wet eyes. "When did you get home?"

"This morning. As soon as I got your letter about the Pied Piper, I got a weekend pass." She squatted in front of me and studied my face. "Werner told me about your mother and your father's arrest. And the doctor, too. I'm so upset, Sophie."

I glanced around for a private spot and pointed to a broad shade tree a dozen meters away. She pushed me there and settled herself on a wooden bench, placed her hand over mine and waited. I soaked in the sight of her pale skin, her silvery eyes, and her short, dark curls for the first time in, how long – four or five weeks? How could she look peaceful and unchanged when my world was so different?

For the next hour or so, I told Rennie all that had happened since I last saw her – the hidden photos, the talent show, the poster, the treason charges – well, everything. She went inside a couple of times, once to get a drink of water and a clean handkerchief and a second time to retrieve Papa's notes and the infamous poster from under my mattress. As she'd done before, she mostly let me talk.

When I was finished, she wiped her tears and smiled at me. "Maybe we can stop the Piper together," her smile spread into a grin, "and break his flute. Remember? I've always wanted to do that."

"I remember. But your brother's not the only problem. Herr Doktor Albrecht wants me to take more photos. He hinted that it might help Papa and Doktor Vogel in their trial. I want to help them if I can, but I'm afraid."

"Of what? Of drawing attention to yourself?"

"Yes, but I'm also afraid that if I take more photos, the Party will use them for their propaganda posters again." Rennie nodded, and I knew she understood. "It makes me feel so dirty."

Those words released something inside me, a barrier of some kind. My face flushed and anger crept upward from my gut. "How could your brother do that to me? To any of us here at the hospital? It's not our fault we got sick, that we're crippled. We don't want to be this way." My fingernails dug into my palms. "He took the very thing I love, my photography, and he twisted it. He used my own photos to create something cruel." My voice broke.

Rennie rubbed small circles on my back and murmured soft words of comfort until my tears were spent. Eventually, she whispered, "What would your father tell you to do?"

I'd already thought about that. "Tell the whole truth, take pictures, and follow my heart."

Rennie's eyebrows pulled together and made a crease. "So what does your heart tell you to do?"

I sighed. "I know I need to do *something*, but I don't know what. And it needs to be done before Klaus gets home."

"Let's think this through." That's all I'd been doing, but I let her think for a while. Finally she said, "Werner brought you only a few of the photos you'd taken? He kept some?"

"He must have. And he gave at least two of them to the Party."

"If you had the prints, he couldn't use them to make another poster."

"I'd need the negatives too. Then I could be sure they wouldn't be printed again."

"My mother cleans offices at night, and Werner's taking Anna to the cinema this evening," Rennie said softly, tilting her face toward me. The thought of Werner and Anna as boyfriend and girlfriend made me wrinkle my nose, but Rennie continued as if she hadn't noticed. "That'll leave me alone for a few hours. If he kept the photos and the negatives, I can find them."

"What if he catches you?"

"Our flat is small. There aren't many places to hide things." She sounded quite sure of herself.

"What if the photos aren't there? What if he took them to the Youth office or gave the negatives to the Party already?"

She shrugged. "Then you're no worse off than you are now. But if he didn't, there's a chance I could find them and then," she stopped short. "Do you want me to destroy them?"

I shook my head. "No." That would be like burning books. "Just bring them to me."

"What will you do with them?"

"Well, maybe I can send them to London, to the contact my father used. Except I'm not sure who that is." I paused. "Until I figure that out, I'll keep them under my mattress with all my other personal things."

"Is that safe? You know, anyone can go in the ward and lift your mattress and…"

133

"I know," I snapped, "but I really don't have much choice. There's no privacy here." A large unplanned tear coursed down my cheek. I pushed it away.

Rennie opened her mouth to speak but abruptly stopped. When she began again, her voice was soft and sad. "There's a problem. My train leaves tomorrow at noon, so I'm going to the Bahnhof right after Mass." She placed her hands in her lap and stared at them. "I won't have time to bring you the photos before I leave."

My heart sank. "Oh." We sat quietly until I said, "You tried. That means a lot."

Voices on the porch drew our attention. Staff members gestured to their watches as they spoke to patients and guests. Visitation was almost over.

"Thanks for coming all the way here to see me." I hugged her. "And thanks for trying to help. You're such a good friend."

She returned my squeeze and blinked a couple times. Two staff members moved toward us, and Rennie stood to go. Suddenly, she turned to me, her face transformed by a wide grin. "The pickle jar. We'll break the Pied Piper's flute with the pickle jar." She left the hospital grounds with a definite skip in her step.

Good old Rennie.

# Chapter Eleven
# Develop

## 4 July, Monday

I studied my reflection in the long mirror at the end of the parallel bars. A metal and leather contraption surrounded my scrawny right leg, lending support from my foot to mid-thigh. My own brace, one I'd be using for years. Maybe forever.

Gisela stood behind me smiling. "You've come a long way, Sophie Adler," she said to my reflection. "How does the brace feel?"

"Good. More sturdy than the temp." I looked at my image again and sighed. "Do all braces look this way?"

The physio cocked her head. "How's that?"

"Ugly and clumsy like this."

She placed her hand on top of mine as I held the parallel bars. "It may not be pretty, Sophie, but it'll get the job done."

Another change I'd have to get used to. What else could I do?

"Take a couple steps," she urged, grasping the belt fastened around my waist for security. Step, drag. Step, drag. The brace was heavy and inflexible. "Try lifting it up from here." She tapped my hip and I tried again. Step, drag. She shook her head. Step-stumble-drag. The belt held me fast until I regained my balance. Step, hike-step. Step, hike-step. "Better!"

We took several trips up and down the bars while I got used to this different way of walking. I felt stable, secure on my feet, and even let go of the bars to briefly balance hands-free.

Gisela beamed. "Next time, we'll practice with a crutch. I can't say for sure, Sophie, but with hard work and a little luck, you might go home soon."

Go home to what? To Klaus?

While I rested in my wheelchair, Doktor Albrecht entered the room and strode toward me. "Good news, Adler," he bellowed. "You've been given an extraordinary opportunity." He stopped at my side, pulled a folded paper from his chest pocket and read:

*"The HJ will join the people in greeting our Führer during his visit to Munich this Sunday. Please allow leave for Sophie Adler so she can photograph the Youth participation in this event. The two rolls of film given her should be used for this occasion.*
*Sincerely,*
*Scharführer Werner Müller"*

He folded the paper and returned it to his pocket. "Our glorious Führer will be in town for the *Festzug am Tag der Deutschen Kunst,*" the Procession for the Day of German Art. "You're familiar with this celebration?"

I nodded. "My family watched it last year." It was a magnificent procession too, with dozens of floats and hundreds of costumed participants displaying various periods of German history, from ancient to modern. I tapped my feet to the marching bands' music and joined the thousands of spectators waving little handheld flags. I'd been proud to be German.

So much had changed.

The doctor handed me a small booklet. "This describes the procession and the route it will take." *Zweitausend Jahre Deutsche Kultur.* Two Thousand Years of German Culture. "Study it."

"What am I to photograph exactly?"

"The Youth. Some HJ will assist parade participants in the staging area before the procession, others will join the parade. Younger members and BDM will line the route in uniform. Future Youth members will watch the event from their mother's arms."

I swallowed past the lump in my throat. "What about the procession itself? What about the Führer? Am I to photograph him as well?"

The doctor waved his hands dismissively. "*Nein, nein.* There will be an entire international press corps there. You just photograph the Youth."

The chance I was waiting for. I could be courageous and photograph the whole truth. I flushed with excitement, but then my heart sank. What would happen to Papa and Mutti and Doktor Vogel when the Reich didn't approve of my photos? Would I put them in even more danger? I couldn't bear the guilt.

The procession would have hundreds of participants, thousands of spectators, plus Youth officials, Party officers, SS, and even the Führer himself. That day, all would be seen. I would be completely exposed.

In. Out. In. Out.

Doktor Albrecht narrowed his eyes and moved closer to me. "Perhaps this is the chance you've been waiting for, Adler, the chance to make up for certain failures within your family." His face stayed close to mine, waiting for a response.

I shook his hand. What else could I do?


The booklet showed that the parade route wound through the heart of the city, in and among a number of Party buildings and sites known for their historical or artistic significance. I opened the route map for the hundredth time when it finally sunk in. The English Garden Park.

Of course! Since the procession started in front of the art museum, the staging area for the participants had to be right behind it in the park. Youth would be milling around in the park, waiting for their group's turn in the parade. That would create casual moments, times when people let their guard down. Maybe I'd see something worth photographing.

The park was home to the pickle jar. With any luck, Rennie had found my missing photos and negatives and stashed them there before she left town. I might be able to take photos and get back what was mine the same afternoon.

I started to formulate my plan. Since the park was several kilometers away, I'd need the streetcar to get there. My wheelchair couldn't go on the streetcar, so I'd be walking all day with that big clumsy brace. Even though I'd only practiced with it once, I'd use one of the metal forearm crutches Elisabeth's father made from old steel pipes. It was heavier than the usual wooden crutch, but I liked its sturdy support.

Once the procession started, I'd be out on my feet constantly to get photos. I'd probably have to rest a lot, leaning against buildings or sitting on benches. I hoped I'd be strong enough for all that walking.

Then my gut twisted. I couldn't plan my shots. The what and when and where of the day were unknown. And once I used the film, then what? I couldn't let Werner develop it. If he saw the shots I hoped to get, I'd be in trouble like Papa.

When it came right down to it, I knew what I wanted to do, but I had absolutely no idea how to make it happen. And there was no one I could ask for help.

## 10 July, Sunday

Rennie was right – nothing was really private in the ward, especially since I'd be gone all afternoon.

I took the rosary and the letters from Erich from under my pillow and tucked them in my pocket. Next, I loaded film in my camera and snugged the extra roll of film in the camera bag. Then I lifted my mattress and grabbed the letters from Papa and the photos of my friends from the hospital and tucked them in the bag as well.

All that was left under my mattress was the poster. I stared at it, again sickened that my beloved photos had been twisted and misused. The thought that dozens or even hundreds of copies of this blatant lie hung all over Germany – I couldn't bear it.

Anger and guilt and shame rose inside me, overwhelming me, smothering me under a dark heavy blanket. I wanted to push out from beneath it, free myself of its crushing weight. I raced to the bathroom and tore the poster in half then in half again and again, gaining the force and speed that comes with outrage, until bits of paper smaller than my thumbnail filled the bottom of the trash can. I stared, panting.

One of the bits clearly showed Elisabeth's tin foil tiara. Sickened, I grabbed a cup, filled it with water and poured, watching the tiara and its surrounding poster pieces darken and soften. Then I poured more and more and reached inside the bin and stirred until the whole sodden mass was an unidentifiable blob. Then I scrubbed my hands until they were red and wrinkled. I vowed to never feel that dirty again.

When I got back to the ward room, raindrops chased each other down the ward windows. I tried to convince myself I could walk in the rain, that it would be all right, but my resolve was crumbling fast under the weight of my anxious doubts.

Anna was there. "I'll be your escort today," she announced, smiling. I gasped before I could stop myself. Her smile faded and she left as abruptly as she'd arrived.

I should have expected an escort. I was a fourteen-year-old girl with polio. It wouldn't be appropriate to open the hospital doors and let me go. But how could I take the pictures I hoped to take with her breathing down my neck, and in the rain to boot?

I closed my eyes. "Dear God, I've asked you for courage and I've got a little. But today I need a lot. This is going to be hard. Please give me the courage to show the whole truth. Amen." I again hoped for something that felt divine, some surge of power. But I didn't feel any different.

The rain had slowed to a drizzle by noon when I met Anna at the hospital entrance. "Do you have your camera and film?"

I patted the bag. "Keeping it dry." I loosened a strap that attached the metal pipe crutch to the back of my chair and used the crutch to stand. In no time, I adjusted my hooded poncho around my shoulders so it covered me and the camera bag completely.

"Why are you standing?"

"To get on the streetcar," I answered simply. "My wheelchair can't go."

She shook her head, lips pursed. "Gisela tells me you aren't ready to walk all day."

"It'll be hard but I can use my crutch…"

"We've arranged other transportation. Sit."

I was grateful I didn't have to walk, but I wondered what the other transportation might be. Anna pushed me across the bumpy sidewalk and through the parking lot until we approached a black sedan. A figure stepped out.

"Werner!"

In. Out. In. Out.

He kept his distance but peered at me and spoke in his usual whine. "Certainly," he said. "I wouldn't miss it." He smiled at Anna. She took his arm and gave him a peck on the cheek.

Remarkable. I'd never seen anyone touch him before, not even his mother. Maybe Anna had broken through that shell. I wondered what Rennie would say.

"Oh, Werner, such an exciting day," Anna gushed.

My insides churned, but I stayed quiet. I transferred into the back seat, readjusted my poncho and camera bag, and tucked my crutch at my feet. Once my wheelchair was stowed in the trunk, the Party loyalists climbed in the front.

# Chapter Twelve
## Flash

I gazed out the car window, soaking in the sights and sounds I'd missed during my weeks in the hospital. Raindrop speckled signs advertised specials at a few eateries, but most businesses were closed. Church bells pealed from nearly every block we passed, and some pedestrians hurried under umbrellas to answer their call. Munich looked and sounded as it had on a thousand other Sundays. It was home.

Individual buildings and entire streets were decked out for the weekend-long arts festival. Some hung the blue and white diamonded Bavarian flag or the striped German national flag, and a few shops showed the flag of the city of Munich. Nearly all also showed the red and black flag of the Party, the swastika, or a picture of the Führer. Their statement was clear – they were Bavarians, they were Müncheners, but they also supported the Party. Or at least they were going along with the Party, like everyone else. Blurring into the background.

Funny. I'd been content in the background too until polio threw me into the spotlight. In a few months time, I'd lost my ability to walk, my parents, and many of my friends. My privacy was gone, and my only productive work, photography, had been misused and turned against me by people I should have been able to trust.

I didn't believe what Doktor Albrecht said. If the Party decided my parents and the doctor were the enemy, nothing I would do this day or any day would help them. Their fate was sealed. That knowledge smacked me full in the gut and I doubled over, reeling.

I wanted to pound my fists and scream about the injustice. But with Werner and Anna right in front of me, what was the point? I'd accomplish nothing and I'd suffer the same fate as the others. I took a deep breath and was amazed at what followed – for the first time in ages, I felt calm and clear-headed.

I wasn't responsible for my loved ones' fate.

That knowledge left me strangely free. I only had to think about me, what I wanted to do, what I hoped to accomplish. The punishment for my actions, if there were any, would fall only on me.

Deep in my gut, a new more positive sense slipped into the empty space once filled with my anxiety. The flush in my face and quickening of my pulse told me – I was excited. The unknown was a challenge, and I'd have to cope. I would cope. I tapped my hand rhythmically against my thigh, my energy rising.

I wasn't powerless. I could do something. I had to stay ready and open to opportunity.

As we neared the parade route, the streets clogged and sidewalks crowded with pedestrians. We pulled over at an intersection and Anna faced me, gesturing out the window. "The press corps is here from all over Europe. They'll see for themselves how strong and unified we Germans are." A knot of suited men, each with a white ID tag dangling from a hat brim and a camera hanging by a neck strap, watched Anna step from our car.

Werner walked around and opened my door. "Come meet these men, Adler."

I slid over and grabbed my crutch, positioned it under me, locked my brace, and stood. I walked slowly to the men, unsure of what I was supposed to say or do. They smiled and a couple of them tipped their hats. One, a short man in a bright green vest, seemed familiar.

Werner saluted and spoke first. *"Heil Hitler."* None returned his greeting, they just nodded. "May I present Anna Albrecht, a nurse at a hospital here in Munich." A student nurse really, but I didn't correct him. The men bobbed their heads in greeting. Then he gestured at me. "And the young photographer, Sophie Adler."

I stuck out my hand and mumbled, *"Gruß Gott,"* and we shook all the way around.

The Scharführer ignored my use of the traditional Bavarian greeting and continued. "As you can see, the Reich uses the talents of all its citizens. Everyone does their part for the Fatherland." His eyes shifted meaningfully to my brace and my crutch before he continued. "Rumors of exclusion of," his voice took on that typical whine, "of certain types have been greatly exaggerated."

So that was it. I was on display. Exhibit number one: the crippled girl who can still be useful to Greater Germany. I turned to him, my mouth open, but I couldn't speak.

The men shifted as if they were uncomfortable, but that green-vested man scribbled furiously.

Werner continued. "Today, Adler will photograph the future of the Fatherland, our Youth. That frees you men to focus on the procession and its presentation of two thousand years of German history. And of course, you'll want to photograph our glorious Führer himself."

He saluted, snapped his heels, and climbed back in the car. Anna saluted and got in the passenger side, leaving me alone on the sidewalk with the press.

I started my slow plod toward the car, that earlier surge of positive feeling slipping away fast. He'd used me again.

"Allow me to get the door for you," someone said in halting German. It was the short man with the green vest, walking toward me with his bowler hat askew and a broad smile on his face. He had a decided limp, and I wondered briefly if a crutch like mine might help him walk better. He was so familiar, and yet... Between his own uneven stride and his haste, he jostled my poncho and bumped into my crutch, knocking both of us off-balance. He fumbled for my arm to stabilize me, and then apologized for his clumsiness in some combination of German and English.

"*Danke.*" I struggled to find my voice and settled into the back seat. As we pulled away from the curb, he stared after us. Gradually, his vest shrank to a green dot, and I lost sight of him in the crowd.

Energy drained from me like water from a bathtub, leaving me cold and shivering with uncertainty. "I want to go home," I announced weakly, surprising myself. "It's been months."

Werner glanced at me in his rearview mirror and his voice took on that annoying whine. "We have no time for this." I didn't respond, but Anna leaned closer and whispered to him. He turned to her. "Anna, you know how important this day is to me, to my future," he said. "I must make sure..." Anna gave him a look that asked for sympathy. He glanced at his watch. "I'll give you fifteen minutes."

The car came to a halt in front of my family's bakery. A sign in the store window read: **Owners on holiday. Reopen 15 July.** I shuddered.

Werner asked, "You have a key, yes?" I nodded. "Go put on your uniform. Wear it while you photograph today."

I reached for some courage. "Scharführer, you and Helga told me I'm not even in BDM..." I started.

A man across the street called, "Werner!" The Youth leader smiled broadly, exited the car, and crossed to greet him. Ignoring me completely, Anna followed. All three lit up cigarettes and began to chat.

On my own. I trudged to the bakery door and with one turn of the key, entered.

Hot, stale air whooshed past me, bringing with it the tang of rancid fruit. A thin layer of gray-white dust coated the empty display case. I walked past the service counter and the cash register and into the work area that had been my parents' domain. A few sacks of flour and sugar remained on the shelves, chewed with irregular holes and leaking bits of white into soft mounds on the floor. Tiny black droppings dotted tin baking pans and wooden work tables. Without Papa's hearty laugh or Mutti's stern orders, the whole bakery felt hollow and lonely, filled only with mice and sadness.

My clumsy shoes and heavy crutch echoed through the empty work area as I headed toward the stairs that led to our second floor flat. More than anything, I wanted to sit in my own bedroom, listen to Mozart on the Victrola, look through Papa's books, see and smell

147

and touch all the things that made our home, well, home. I stopped at the base of the long flight of stairs. It may as well have been the Matterhorn. No way I could drag my heavy brace up those steps and still have energy for what I needed to do.

Complete despair overwhelmed me, squashing whatever bits of hope I'd had. I dropped my head against the newel post and sobbed, "*Gott im Himmel,* Dear God in heaven, what am I supposed to do? Help me, please Holy Mother Mary, help me." When I reached under my poncho for my handkerchief, a small rectangular card pulled out with it.

**Peter Massey**
**German correspondent**
**London**

I wiped my eyes, flipped the card over, and read the words scrawled on the back.

*You resemble your father.*
*At your service,*
*PM*

My heart pounded. The man with the green vest and the limp must have tucked the card into my pocket when he bumped me. I stumbled to a chair to collect my thoughts.

I flipped the card over several times, rereading the words. His name and face were familiar. Then I had it. I'd met him the night of the first aid demonstration. Didn't he say he knew Papa? Yes, he even knew the bakery and he said that... wait a minute... he said that he and Papa used the same film developer in Schwabing.

Doktor Vogel had used the developer in Schwabing also.

My heart leapt. That man with the green vest, that Peter Massey, he was the contact Papa used to get his photos to the London newspaper. He had to be. I closed my eyes and said a prayer of thanks.

I glanced out the front window. Anna and Werner were still smoking and chatting. No way to tell how long I had. My energy returned.

I opened a cabinet, took out a couple muffin tins, and reached back in. Running my hand against the rear wall, I tripped a tiny latch and opened a panel. From inside, I removed the old cigar box which held the bakery's proceeds between visits to the bank. Forty-seven mark plus change. Quite a lot of money, probably a week's worth of sales. No doubt Mutti didn't get a chance to settle accounts before she was arrested. I tore a sheet of paper from a receipt pad and scribbled a hasty note.

*I took five mark from the cashbox and pray I can repay it soon.*

*Your Sophie*

I didn't know when my parents would see the note, if ever. No doubt Klaus would read it when he reopened the bakery. But I wasn't going to hide anything anymore.

I placed my note on top of the remaining bills in the cigar box, returned it to its hiding place, and glanced out the window. Werner looked at his watch and at the storefront, shifting his weight as if to start walking toward the bakery. Thankfully, two other people joined their trio. He and Anna stayed there, chatting amiably. I let out a long breath. I tore a second sheet from the receipt pad and wrote.

*Dear Herr Massey,*

*Like my father, I trust you. Enclosed are images of my friends from the polio hospital. Photos like these have been used against us, trying to convince Germans that cripples like us are useless. They mock us with words and cruel images. Who knows what might happen next. I place these precious items with you for safekeeping.*

*The tins contain film shot today. Use the money to develop it. I hope the photos show things the international press corps did not see, ugly things which happen here when outsiders aren't looking. Please show the world.*

*Yours truly,*

*Sophie Adler*

I glanced out the window again – Werner and Anna were walking toward the bakery at a good clip. I stuffed the letter and the money in my camera bag and had just readjusted my poncho when they entered.

While Anna stood in the open doorway and leaned against its frame, watching, Werner marched toward me. "What have you been doing, Adler? Why aren't you in uniform?" He leaned toward me, not close enough to touch of course, but his voice growled. "Didn't I tell you…" he began, shaking a finger.

Anna moved forward, grasped his accusing finger in her hand, and lowered it. "Don't be hard on her. She needs to save her strength." He glared at her but she continued. "Besides, her uniform would be hidden by the rain poncho today."

Anna really confused me. Sometimes I didn't dare turn my back on her. Sometimes, like now, she was on my side.

He ripped his finger from Anna's grip and marched to the sidewalk, wiping it against his pants in a not-too-subtle cleaning gesture.

Anna followed and I locked the door behind us. Once on the sidewalk, he whirled on me. "You didn't do as you were told, Adler," he said, his voice an accusing hiss. "You were given a simple command – put on your uniform. No need to remind you that much depends on your performance." We drove away from my home in total silence.

I closed my eyes, trying to remember which corner the press corps had been on, but it escaped me.

We parked a few blocks from the English Garden. I transferred into my wheelchair and pushed myself, grateful for my hooded poncho in the fine drizzle. Anna smiled and walked alongside her boyfriend as if nothing had happened, but he kept his eyes straight ahead.

"Werner," Anna said, "the procession doesn't start for a couple hours. Want to get something to eat?" He stopped short and stared at her. "What's wrong?" she asked. I pulled up alongside her to listen.

"Something to eat." His tone mocked her request. "You know how critical today is for me, how many will see my work."

After a moment's hesitation, Anna nodded. "Your Youth should be at their best."

He sniffed and pulled into a ridiculously straight pose. "They're the Führer's Youth, Anna. Remember that." I shivered, and not because of the damp weather. He turned to me. "Adler, go take pictures." Then back to Anna. "Watch her," he commanded. "Meet at my car right after the parade." He saluted, spun, and left us on the sidewalk.

Anna returned the salute and watched his retreating figure. "Men," she grumbled. She moved behind my chair and pushed me toward the park, mumbling the whole time about lunch and rain and bossy boyfriends. She slowed only a little for bumps in the sidewalk.

# Chapter Thirteen
## Advance

The drizzle lessened as we threaded our way through thickening crowds of spectators. Vendors hawked balloons, flags, and snacks from pushcarts. A perfect start to my assigned photos. "Please stop," I said at a busy corner. "I see some children." Anna complied but watched my every move, so I was careful not to let her see the papers and photos stuffed in my oversized camera bag. I focused on a small boy as he approached a vendor, a coin in his outstretched hand. The vendor exchanged his coin for a bag of nuts. Click. The boy skipped away, his snack bouncing perilously in a chubby fist. Click.

Anna nodded. Her endorsement was good. With any luck she'd pay less attention to photos I took later. Hopefully I'd find something worth shooting. I tried not to think about my lack of a plan.

And then, there it was. While I was focused on some ladies and their fussing babies, I caught sight of a paper tacked to a pole. It was the familiar rectangular poster, Klaus and Erich on the top, Elisabeth on the bottom.

Seeing the horrid thing out in public shocked me, and I nearly dropped the camera. But after a deep breath or two, I worked the focus dial to draw the image in. Click.

Click again, for good measure.

Papa had taken photos of Jews, showing how they'd become targets. I'd add photos of cripples. They, I mean we, were targets too. The people of England and all the people in the world needed to know. One mistake of sharing your canteen with a sick girl, one illness, one injury, even for a German citizen or former Youth member, and we were written off as useless, same as the Party's other targets.

To avoid Anna's suspicion, I focused on boys in knickers as they chased girls in Sunday dresses. Click.

As Anna pushed me toward the parade route, I noticed another three or four posters. Each time, I asked her to stop. Each time I focused long and captured that poster's horrifying message again. And again.

Even at this celebration of national history and pride, the posters oozed their poison all over Munich. And the people who read those posters, saw those pictures, might actually believe that cripples like us were no good for Germany. That we were useless eaters.

I had to get these images to the free press in England. I had to find Peter Massey.

When Anna and I came off the side street and onto Prinzregenten Strasse across from the art museum, a wall of people blocked our path. She inched me through the dense crowd. I clutched my camera bag against the onslaught of elbows and hips.

The crowd ended abruptly and we faced a row of wooden barricades. "Where are you going?" a brown-shirted officer demanded.

"We're working under the orders of Scharführer Werner Müller," Anna said. "Now let us cross." Her voice had a tone of authority, and without further question the officer slid a barricade aside for us.

We moved into the empty street, all traffic halted in anticipation of the parade. From there I saw the true size of the crowd. As far as the eye could see, people clotted the available space between curbstone and buildings. Thousands and thousands of people pressed together, blurred, fading into an anonymous background. Black, white, and red Party flags sprouted like weeds from every imaginable spot – small ones cradled in hands, large ones draped on buildings, hung from balconies, wrapped around statues. Several groups of uniformed Youth stood along the curb, each member grasping the stick of a tiny Party flag. Click. Click.

We reached the opposite sidewalk, and with it another wall of officers and wooden barricades. We again explained our purpose at the park and we worked our way through a mirror image of that first crowd.

Finally, we entered the staging area for the procession's participants, the leafy refuge of the English Garden Park. Anna's frantic pushing and steering relaxed and her pace slowed. "I can take it from here," I said, and we moved side by side along the paved path.

As I expected, groups of costumed participants had clustered at the park as they readied for the procession. A dozen giggling ladies lounged on plaid blankets beneath a shade tree, their white taffeta dresses draped around their legs, bare feet thrust beside their waiting shoes. Young girls in uniform stood nearby weaving circlets of daisies for the women's hair and wrists. I seemed to be the only photographer in sight. Anna nudged me. Click.

A cluster of men struggled into the cloaks and tunics of ancient Roman soldiers. Two skinny boys in uniform held metallic helmets and shields while the soldiers dressed. The boys fixed their eager gaze first at the armor, then up at the costumed men. Anna pointed. Click.

I wanted to get to the pickle jar. And I had to find Peter Massey and give him the film. I tried to not feel overwhelmed by my own lack of a plan.

We approached a group of a dozen men dressed as tournament knights. Several HJ helped with details of their armored costumes or readied the knights' nearby horses. Click.

One Youth, a tall boy placing a saddle on a horse, caught my eye. Erich. My heart quickened and I wanted to rush to him, but I stopped myself. For the first time ever, I hoped he didn't notice me. I didn't want the distraction.

The horses, obviously accustomed to the noise and fuss involved in parades, waited quietly as the men clanked about. A knight mounted his horse and posed, javelin vertical in his gloved hand. Some women on nearby park benches applauded and ran to surround him. Anna joined the other women gawking at the knight.

That left the benches empty and exposed a plaque I hadn't seen before. *Nur für Arier.* For Aryans only. I made sure Anna's attention was still diverted. Click.

A second vacant bench also had a sign. *Juden sind nicht erwünscht.* Jews not wanted. Click.

Anna started toward me. She must have seen me turning away from the bench because she scowled and hastened her steps. "What did you photograph, Sophie?"

I answered honestly. "The signs. I've never seen them before."

Her scowl deepened. "They've been here for months."

But I hadn't been. Munich had changed. Or more likely, I had changed.

Somewhere down the path, a gruff voice shouted. All heads turned, including mine, to watch dozens of men mount horses and form a line along the path, two abreast. Each man held a tall flagpole bearing the Party's colors, each flag about three meters long and two meters tall. The effect was overwhelming. The men and their horses and even the beauty of the park were lost – the red and black flags were all I could see, snapping like fish in the talons of eagles.

The Führer would already be in the Grandstand, surrounded by Party officials and SS by the dozen. The international press would be somewhere near the Grandstand as well, including Peter Massey. My insides jittered. Unless by chance he was here in the park, I'd be in full view of the Grandstand when I gave Herr Massey the film.

As flag-bearers on horseback moved up the path toward us, Anna pulled my wheelchair back into the grass. Small clusters of spectators stood nearby, obviously enjoying this less structured prelude to the parade. One man hobbled alone through the grass, leaning heavily on a cane. Between the crowd and the irregular surface, he walked slowly, a step-drag pattern much like my own. When he reached the empty bench a half-dozen meters from me, he sort of collapsed into it. In moments though, he straightened and leaned forward with hands atop his cane, watching the approaching riders and smiling.

I wondered if he had polio or if some other disease or injury had left him weak and crippled. Erich approached him and saluted, then spoke and pointed toward the riders. I held my breath and steadied my camera.

The man didn't return the salute but nodded and continued to smile. Erich leaned toward him and said rather loudly, "The flag, sir. You need to stand before the flag."

I focused my camera on the crippled man and drew his image closer. I glanced at Anna beside me, but she was looking at something else. Good. She wouldn't interfere. I faced the bench. Click.

"What's this?" a high-pitched voice said from behind me. Werner strode up the grass past me, toward Erich and the man.

The crippled man continued to sit forward with his hands leaning heavily atop his cane, smiling evenly. "Surely you don't begrudge a weak man his rest," he said.

Werner lifted a polished boot and kicked the cane. Click.

Without the cane's support, the man toppled forward off the bench and landed hard. Blood gushed from his mouth and nose. Click.

Several women in the crowd screamed. Erich gasped and crouched beside the man, cradling his head and pressing a handkerchief to his nose.

Anna stood frozen, staring at the man. I shook her arm. "You're a nurse. That man is bleeding." Her eyes moved from Werner to the man but she remained motionless.

The Youth leader stared at Erich and the man without offering help. Click.

Anna watched her boyfriend as if waiting for him to speak. To give permission?

If she wouldn't help, then I would. I pushed toward the man and Erich glanced up, his face registering recognition and surprise. My hands began to sweat. "What can I do?" I asked him. He was speechless.

Werner turned and snapped his fingers. "Anna," he commanded, "be a nurse." Only then did Anna crouch beside the man.

She made me sick.

The Scharführer's next order was, "Fischer, tend to your own duties."

Erich hesitated, looking from the injured man to Anna, then to his Youth leader and to me. Anna assured him she was in control and Erich said a few words of reassurance to the injured man before he left. Just once, he glanced back at me and smiled. Werner left us moments later.

While all this happened, the flag-bearers had continued up the path at a slow, steady pace past hushed groups of saluting bystanders. The flag-bearers were still a dozen meters away when I pushed a safe distance onto the grass and placed my sweaty, trembling hands on my camera.

The lead rider called, "Halt." The entire company of horses stopped within a pace or two. All movement and sound vanished except the pounding of my heart and the snap, snap, snap of those huge flags.

The rider glowered down at Anna and the man. She seemed to understand what was expected because she lifted under the man's arms to force him to his feet. Someone handed the man his cane and he stood, swaying slightly and obviously dazed, a scarlet-stained handkerchief pressed to his nose and Anna's support around his waist. Click.

Once the riders moved forward, the man collapsed on the bench. Click.

I wondered how soon a "No Cripples Allowed" or "Useless Eaters Forbidden" sign would decorate one of these benches.

Anna handed the man his cane. "Can you walk?"

He nodded and took a step or two, wobbling perilously. She supported under his arm and furrowed her eyebrows, looking at the crowd. "Can someone help?" The people left in the park were mostly costumed participants, all with a job to do. None offered help.

"I think his nose is broken and he might have a concussion," Anna told me. "He needs to go to a hospital. I'll look for an ambulance." Good. She was acting as a nurse again, too.

"I'd only slow you down." I gestured to my wheelchair and Anna nodded. She and the man weren't more than a few faltering steps away when I spun my chair and pushed toward the pickle jar.

Since the path was clogged with costumed people, I was forced to push on the wet grass. That was slow going. I passed a dozen other Youth members, all engaged in various tasks helping parade participants, but I didn't take any more pictures.

The deeper I got into the park the emptier it grew, so a hundred meters in I was again able to use the path. A minute or two later I saw it – the scruffy clump of pine trees. I glanced around. No one in sight. I pushed as quickly as I could to the base.

I lowered myself so my bottom sat on the footrests then brushed away pine needles. I grabbed the lid of the pickle jar and wiggled and pulled, hoping to work the jar free from the soil. No luck. I tried using a stick as a lever, jamming it around the jar and lifting. Still not working. Rennie must have stomped the soil down with her shoes. I needed a better tool, a wider one. I lifted back into my seat and grabbed my pipe crutch from its holder behind the chair, scooted down to the footplate, and used the crutch as the lever. The jar lifted free.

Clods of wet dirt and needles coated both the jar and my hands, so I used my poncho to grasp the damp lid and unscrew it. Inside was an envelope rolled into a half-circle, Rennie's gift to me – eighteen photos plus negatives. Hopefully all the shots her brother had taken from me, including the one of Elisabeth he'd misused. I unfolded the small square of paper tucked inside.

*As I promised.*

Good old Rennie.

Twenty minutes had passed. No doubt Anna was looking for me. I slid Rennie's envelope into the inside pocket of my poncho. Then I rewound the used film in my camera, stashed it in its tin, and pocketed that as well.

In case I decided to take more pictures, I loaded the second roll of film and dropped the empty tin in the bag.

I was proud of the photos I'd taken, ones of the poster and ones that showed how cripples like that poor man and Elisabeth and me were treated by the Reich. My photos were as important as Papa's.

That jittery feeling started in my stomach again. How could I hand the Briton an envelope of photos and a tin of exposed film in front of all those SS? And the Führer himself? I'd be seen. I'd be caught. Which would give my photos to the Party. Which would leave me open to charges of disobeying orders from the Youth leader. I might be charged with treason, as my father and Doktor Vogel had been. All this would have been for nothing.

But I had already made my choice. I remembered Papa saying something about how we must decide if our choice is worth the cost. This choice was worth it, even if my photos didn't get to Peter Massey, to England, to the world. I was trying. I couldn't live with the guilt if I didn't try.

I buried the empty pickle jar, then lifted myself to the wheelchair's seat and turned to hook my crutch to its support strap behind me. A stone's throw away, two people walked down the path – Anna and a young man in an HJ uniform.

"Ah, there you are," the young man said, separating from Anna and striding toward me at a brisk pace.

It was Klaus.

It was too late to disguise the mud under my nails and on my clothes, too late to hide the freshly turned earth behind me. Rennie's note still lay in my lap. I closed my fist over top of it.

"You're easy to follow. Wet wheels leave tracks." He picked a dandelion, handed it to me, and kissed the top of my head. "Good to see you, little cat." His eyes scanned me. "Aren't you a little old to play in the mud?"

My throat closed tight. I didn't need another loyal Party member watching my every move. In. Out. In. Out.

I squared my shoulders and tried to look brave and confident but my insides tumbled, unsure which way was up.

Anna stood behind him, hands on hips and eyebrows creased together. "What have you been doing, Sophie? Why didn't you wait for me by the bench?"

Before I could answer, Klaus took control. "The Scharführer arranged an early release for me. That way I could be here for your big day. A nice surprise, huh?" He squatted and put his hands on the sides of my wheelchair. "Now that our parents are," he paused for effect, "are away, I'm your guardian. So tell me, what did we catch you doing, little cat?" He glanced from my clothes to the obviously moved dirt behind me and then to my filthy closed fist. He snatched my hand and squeezed it, turning the palm upward to reveal the small note. "What's this?" His eyes moved from the note to the dirt and to me again. Then he threw back his head and laughed. "Are you still passing notes with your little boyfriend?"

"What?"

"Erich Fischer. I saw him a few minutes ago, working the horses up at the front of the park."

So Klaus still thought Erich and I were sending notes. I'd never corrected that thought of his. My heart thudded and I smiled a little. "I saw Erich today, too."

"I'll bet you did," he said, laughing again. "Anna, look at this." He handed her the note and quoted it in a mocking tone. "As I promised. How sweet."

"What does this mean, Sophie?" Anna shook the note with one hand while the other stayed firmly on her hip.

Klaus waved off her doubts. "Isn't it obvious? She had a few minutes to spare and hurried here to dig up the note from her sweetheart. Young romantic foolishness."

Anna glanced at her watch. "There's no time for this," she announced. "The procession is underway."

I gestured to the nearby stream. "I need to rinse my hands so I don't get mud on the camera."

"*Ja, ja. Mach schnell!* Hurry up!"

I pushed across the grass to the stream's edge and lowered myself to the footplate as I'd done before. I glanced over my shoulder. Anna dug in the loose dirt and Klaus stood watching her, arms crossed. All they would find was an empty pickle jar.

But who was I kidding? Loyal Party members would hover over me all day. Incriminating film was in my pocket; personal letters and photos were in my camera bag. I had no idea how to find a contact who didn't know I was looking for him.

My chance of success was nil. My chance of being caught was pretty darn good.

# Chapter Fourteen
## Focus

I slipped the poncho over my head to rinse it and patted the buttoned pocket, feeling for the telltale lumps. The photos were still there. I scooped small amounts of water over the oilcloth fabric and rubbed a little to rinse the dirt, then shook it and slipped it back on. Still stalling, I lifted myself to the seat and glanced over my shoulder at my escorts. Klaus held the empty pickle jar.

I took a deep breath, summoning the courage to meet my fate with my head high. As I began to turn away from the stream, one tire struck a rock and the chair jostled, knocking my crutch out of its holder. I leaned over to get it and noticed – above the crutch's muddy rubber tip was a small crescent of clean, shiny metal. Curious, I grabbed the tip and wiggled it. With a few tugs, the tip came right off.

The crutch was a hollow metal tube. Of course – it was an old steel pipe. A plan came into focus.

I glanced over my shoulder again. Erich had joined Anna and Klaus and the three talked animatedly. I had a few moments.

With the crutch tucked in my lap, I curled Rennie's envelope into a tight circle and shoved it deep in the hollow. The letters and pictures from the camera bag followed two or three at a time and then at last, that tin of newly shot film. It all fit, barely, but in less than a minute, I pressed the rubber tip on and turned to fasten the crutch behind my chair.

165

Anna and Klaus approached, Erich close at their heels. My heart pounded. "Sophie," Erich said with a tight smile, "you're looking well. It's good to see you out of the hospital." His eyes scanned my face anxiously.

I pulled my gaze away. He couldn't distract me, not now.

Anna moved behind my chair and started to push. "We'll have to talk while we walk. You're late." Klaus and Erich fell into step on either side of me.

I glanced to the back of my chair. My crutch was there. If only I could find Peter Massey, I could...

"The Scharführer saw you taking pictures, Sophie," Klaus said evenly, breaking into my thoughts.

In. Out. In. Out. "Of course I took pictures. That's my assignment. Photograph the Youth."

Anna let out some breath between pursed lips. "You know perfectly well what he means. You took pictures of the benches and that crippled man. We all saw you."

"Is that true, Sophie?" Klaus asked. His voice was gentle and kind, like Papa's. But I knew he was only trying to get what he wanted.

I had to hang on until I could find Peter Massey and give him...

"Sophie, stop daydreaming," Klaus said more harshly. "Erich tells me he has never left you notes in a jar."

Erich stared at the ground in front of him. He'd probably answered Klaus' questions honestly, not knowing that the truth would leave me exposed. Poor guy. Now he knew.

"So tell me, little cat," Klaus said. "What are you up to?"

166

Erich lifted his head, and I saw the worry in his face. "Sophie, the Scharführer wants the film."

Klaus wagged his finger at me, mocking me with his disapproval. "Now, little sister, you'll see that sneaking around doesn't pay. All those years of eavesdropping and sending secret notes to who-knows-who... that's all about to end."

Erich stayed quiet but I felt the magnetic pull of his gaze on my every expression and movement. I wondered if he would help with my impromptu plan.

Anna hurried me along the path until it again became crowded with participants, then she bumped my wheelchair onto the grass. Hundreds of feet and hooves had created divots in the turf and pushing my chair there was difficult. A half-dozen times my wheels stuck abruptly, jerking me forward and making Anna stagger.

"Let me do that," Klaus snapped. He brushed Anna aside and tipped my chair back so my front wheels rose in the air. I held the seat for dear life as Klaus pushed me in that ridiculous tipped position. When we finally left the park and reached the street, he dropped my front wheels to the sidewalk, sending rattles up to my teeth. I peered over my shoulder. My crutch was still there.

"Where are we going?" I hollered over the cheers and applause of the parade-watching crowd.

"To give the Scharführer his film," Erich answered; then he stopped. "Where did he say we should meet him?"

"Across from the Grandstand," Klaus said.

Erich turned his head side to side, looking confused. "Which way?"

Klaus huffed. "You push her, Erich. I'll lead. Anna, walk with me to clear the way for the wheelchair."

After shifting positions, our little foursome of people and wheelchair moved through the immense crowd. All I could see were Klaus and Anna's backs and hundreds of hips and elbows. A couple times, Erich bent low behind me and said something but his words were lost in the surrounding din.

We continued that way for a block or two. At an intersection when Erich tipped me backward to lower down a curb, we stopped abruptly. I peered over my shoulder, my heart in my throat. Erich stooped to the sidewalk and returned holding my crutch. "Can you hold this?" he said. "I keep bumping it."

I clasped my hands around the cool metal cylinder, placed the rubber tip on my footplate, and pressed down. The tip was intact. My secret stash was safe inside.

As he pushed again Erich's voice came close to my ear, and this time I heard him. "I can get them away for a few minutes. Would that help?"

I was stunned. "Help?"

He bent even closer and I tried to focus, tried to separate his voice from the crowd noise, separate his warm and earthy scent from the sweaty stench of so many people. "You're hiding something important, right?"

I caught my breath.

"I don't know what you're up to, but I'm sure you'll have no regrets." He sounded pleased, proud.

A thrill ran through me. I turned my head a bit more to catch a glimpse of his face, so close to my own.

He repeated, "Would it help to get them away from you?"

"Yes. Can you do that?"

He nodded but we couldn't say more because we'd arrived. We were across the street from a large covered stand of bleachers. The Grandstand.

Party flags fell from the roof edge. Members of the HJ and SS sat in uniformed groups in the bleachers like dark spots on a leopard. Several rows of bleachers held only a dozen figures completely surrounded by black coats. The Führer and his top aides. I drew in a breath.

A voice whined behind me and my chair spun around. "Ah, there you are." Werner gazed down his long, thin nose at me.

Judging by his tone and his clenched jaw, he was terribly angry. My decisions faltered. "You photographed that man's, shall we say, unfortunate fall," he stated. "Tsk, tsk. Unauthorized photographs with the Party's film." He grabbed my camera bag. Erich started toward me, probably to protect me, but when the strap slid easily over my head, he stopped. Werner opened the bag and pulled out the camera.

Instinctively, I reached for it and as I did, I saw something. A green vest near the curb not a dozen meters away. Peter Massey!

I needed to make a ruckus so he'd look my way. "Please," I said louder than needed, "my father gave me that camera. It was a gift." The crowd noise drowned my words.

Werner ignored my plea and stepped away so the camera was out of my reach. He fiddled with the buttons until he opened the back, grabbed the film inside and

169

yanked. It spun free of its spindles and fell to the ground, untethered as an autumn leaf. I watched it blow into the gutter and partially submerge in a puddle. "There are your precious photos, Adler. Exposed and ruined."

The film fluttered not far from Peter Massey. He turned to figure out its source.

I rested my fingers on the cool metal of my crutch. Still there. Werner had only exposed and ruined film I hadn't used yet. I was pleased. So far.

He rummaged through the camera bag and pulled out the empty film tin. He peeked inside, flipped the bag upside down and shook. Nothing. "I gave you two rolls of film for today." Suspicion was plain in his voice. "Where's the second roll?"

Anna straightened, obviously looking for a compliment. "She wouldn't have had time to shoot a second roll. I only left her alone a few minutes."

"You what?" the Youth leader screeched. "You left her alone when I ordered you to watch her?"

Peter Massey took a couple lurching steps toward us.

Anna hesitated and her voice broke a bit. "Don't be mad, Werner. The crippled man was hurt. I'm a nurse and I had to…"

Werner trembled and I thought he might strike her. She stopped speaking and slowly reached out her fisted hand and turned it palm up. The tiny note from Rennie lay there, crumpled. He read it, and then frowned at me. "You and my sister have been sending notes?"

Klaus, Erich, and Anna exchanged glances. "That was written by Renate?" Klaus asked, obviously surprised.

170

"*Ja,*" he said. "I know her handwriting. She and Sophie have been friends for many years. Always scheming and plotting, those two."

I smiled. Even at a time like this, thinking about Rennie made me smile.

"Where did you find this?" he asked, shaking the note.

"In the park," Anna answered. "From what we could tell, Sophie dug up an old jar and buried it again. We checked – it was empty."

Werner stuffed the note in his pocket. "Little girl nonsense. Renate is fifty kilometers away. What I want to know is," at this he leaned over me, "where is the other roll of film?"

I didn't answer. Peter Massey walked another meter or two toward us before his way was blocked by a knot of BDM girls waving flags.

"You pledged loyalty to the Party, to the Führer," he said to me, his tone threatening, pressing fists into hips and straightening to his full height. He towered over me, not hard to do since I sat in a wheelchair. "You of all people know the penalty for traitors. Do you denounce your pledge?"

"You and Helga told me I'm not a member anymore. Remember? There's no place in BDM for someone like me." A strange sensation – a rush of heat to my cheeks and heart at the same time, some combination of pride and terror – surged through me.

Erich fidgeted and studied me, worry plain on his face. I shifted my eyes down the curb, and Erich followed my gaze to where Peter Massey struggled through the crowd. Erich's eyes widened briefly, then he turned to the others. "She must have left the film at the park," Erich said abruptly. "Why don't you three," he gestured to Werner, Anna, and Klaus, "go look for it. I'll wait here with Sophie."

My heart leapt but almost instantly, my hopes were crushed. "No, you three go," Werner said. "When you find it, bring it to me."

Erich's shoulders slumped as if air had been knocked out of him. He opened his mouth to argue, but I shook my head. With Werner's mind made up, there was no point. Erich had to go.

Peter Massey stopped his movement toward us and once again faced the procession, photographing.

"And Anna," Werner continued, "shame on you, letting a cripple get the best of you." Anna hung her head.

"Let's bring Sophie with us," Klaus suggested. "She can lead us to the film."

"No!" the Youth leader snapped. "This slippery girl stays with me."

I tried to keep my voice light. "Be back in fifteen or twenty minutes so you don't miss anything you'll regret." Erich's dark eyes widened and he gave a crisp nod and a hint of a smile. The three of them turned and headed toward the park and in moments, they blended into the crowd.

I was on my own.

# Chapter Fifteen
# Exposure

Werner grabbed my wheelchair and spun it so I faced the Grandstand. "Our Führer is right across the street, Adler," he announced, "and his men have binoculars. They can see everything. So no funny business. Understand?"

I nodded and pretended to watch the procession. Peter Massey was close, so close. He didn't know I had photos to give him.

A crazy plan formed in my head, part desperation, part fear, part hope. I risked being seen – no, I definitely would be seen. By the Youth leader. By dozens of SS. By the Führer himself. But it had to be done. It was my only chance.

As the moments passed, I sensed Werner relax behind me. I turned my chair a bit to my left where I could see Peter Massey still photographing. I tipped my face to the Youth leader. "Scharführer?" He leaned toward me, drawing close in an effort to hear me over the roar of the crowd. I whispered, so soft as to be barely audible. As I hoped, he pulled a bit closer to try to hear. I whispered a second time, and again, he drew closer. Once I was able to feel his breath hot against my cheek, I knew he was close enough. That's when I did it.

I sneezed in his face.

Just as Rennie described months earlier, Werner's hands flew to cover his face. He fumbled for a handkerchief, sputtering, spitting, cursing me, and wiping furiously. That gave me a few seconds of freedom.

I pushed hard. "Herr Massey!" I called. "Peter Massey!" The Briton glanced my way, smiled, and started to walk toward me.

But I was too close to the curb. My right wheels bumped to the street below. For a ridiculous moment the chair almost balanced, two wheels on the sidewalk and two on the street. Then it tipped over sideways. I threw my crutch forward and watched it skitter in the gutter toward Herr Massey just as my right shoulder crashed to the pavement.

People screamed. Voices gathered around me. I blinked a few times, trying to focus as I gasped in pain. Peter Massey had stepped off the curb, picked up my crutch, and was moving toward me in his odd, lurching style. I wanted him to take the crutch and leave, but there he was, returning it to me. Didn't he understand?

"Thought you could get away that easily?" Werner hissed as he squatted beside me, his face now a healthy distance away.

Two middle-aged women came over to help. "Does the girl need an ambulance?" one asked as the other righted my empty wheelchair.

Werner's voice took on a falsely pleasant tone, and he straightened. "*Nein, danke*, she's with me." He scooped me up from the pavement and plopped me roughly in my wheelchair. Knives seemed to pierce my right shoulder and I gasped and cradled my arm against my chest. Probably broken. "I'll get her to a doctor." The women murmured their good wishes and disappeared into the crowd.

Herr Massey stood a meter or so in front of me, watching intently, holding my crutch and its hidden stash. I wanted him to understand.

"I guess you won't be pushing for a while, not with that shoulder." Werner scanned the crowd and gestured at a pimply teen in an HJ uniform. "Find the ambulance." The Youth saluted and left, and that's when Werner faced me and hissed. "I'll escort you to the hospital. When the doctors are finished, you can tell me where the film is. Or perhaps you'd care to tell the SS?"

Herr Massey's eyebrows shot up, creasing his forehead. The crutch was still clasped in his hand.

I focused on the Briton. "I cannot finish my assignment," I said wincing.

Werner waved a hand in the space between Herr Massey and me. "This is no time for the press."

I stayed focused on Herr Massey. "I was to photograph the Youth." I darted my eyes to the crutch and lifted my chin several times. I hoped the gesture would say, "Take that, please."

Werner looked from me to the Briton, then at the small crowd who watched our little drama. "Don't you understand? The press isn't needed here. This cripple is hurt, and we are waiting for the ambulance." He shifted, obviously anxious to get Herr Massey away.

"Can you complete the assignment for me?" I asked, my eyes moving between the crutch and Herr Massey's face.

He tipped his head and studied me. Again I pushed my chin toward the crutch in his hand. Suddenly his eyes widened. Understanding at last. He gave a quick nod and clamped the crutch's cuff onto his forearm as if it were his own. "Always glad to help a fellow photographer."

I watched Herr Massey work his way through the throngs of spectators, his bright green vest no longer lurching thanks to the stability of my crutch. Once and only once, he looked back at me and our eyes met. He lifted the crutch, tapped it, and waved. Weakly, I raised my good arm in acknowledgement.

In minutes, I'd be on my way to the hospital. What would happen to me was anyone's guess. But my photos were on their way to England. Maybe, just maybe, the world would see the whole truth.

I closed my eyes. "Dear God, thank you for the courage."

I had nothing to feel guilty about. I had no regrets. I had done what I could.

# Glossary

**Altstadt**: Old Town. The Medieval center of Munich.

**Anschluss**: the occupation and annexation of Austria by Nazi Germany.

**Auf Weidersehen**: Goodbye.

**Bahnhof**: Train station.

**Bitte**: please.

**BDM, Bund Deutsche Mädel**: branch of the Hitler Youth for girls ages 14-18.

**Danke**: thank you.

**Deutschland**: Germany.

**Eins, zwei, drei**: One, two, three.

**Fatherland**: Germany.

**Frau and Fräulein**: Mrs. and Miss.

**Führer**: leader, used as Adolf Hitler's title during the Nazi era.

**Great War**: World War I.

**Gruβ Gott**: God's greeting, the traditional Bavarian 'hello.'

**Guten Abend**: Good evening.

**Heil Hitler**: Hail Hitler, the accepted and expected greeting to be used by all Germans during the Nazi era.

**Herr**: Mister.

**HJ, Hitlerjugend, Hitler Youth**: Both the overall organization for children ages 10-18 and the branch of Youth specifically for boys ages 14-18.

**Ja**: yes.

**Jungmädel**: Branch of the Hitler Youth for girls ages 10-14. All transfers to BDM occurred on April 20th, Hitler's birthday, once a girl reached age 14.

**Karnevale**: an annual celebration the day before Lent, known in some other countries as Fat Tuesday.

**Königsplatz**: a large open plaza in Munich, site of many Nazi Party rallies.

**Mach schnell**: hurry.

**Marienplatz**: a large pedestrian plaza in Munich, bordered by shops, restaurants, and the Old and New Town Halls.

**Mensch Ärgere Dich Nicht**: A German board game similar to Parcheesi.

**Müncheners**: Residents of Munich.

**Mutti**: mom.

**Nein**: no.

**Oktoberfest**: a huge annual multi-day celebration which originated in Munich. Smaller versions are celebrated as harvest festivals in many locations worldwide.

**Party**: the Nationalsozialistische deutsche Arbeiterpartei (NSDAP) – National Socialist German Worker's Party, commonly called the Nazi Party.

**Reich**: Empire. The Nazis called their plan for Germany's expansion the Third Reich or the Thousand Year Reich.

**SA**: Sturmabteilung. An independent, brazen group of Nazi soldiers known for their street thug style, SA were also called storm troopers or brown shirts.

**SS**: Schutzstaffel. Known for their all-black uniforms, they acted as the Nazi Party's notorious "Protection Squadron."

**Scharführer**: Master Sergeant.

**Schwabing**: a Munich neighborhood.

**Schwärzwalder Kirchtorte**: Black Forest cherry cake.

**Star on clothing**: The Star of David, a yellow six-pointed star sewn on clothing or worn on an armband, used to identify people with Jewish heritage.

**Strasse**: street.

**Uhr**: literally hour. Similar to military time, Germans use a 24-hour clock, so 15 Uhr is 3 pm.

**Useless eaters**: Term used to disparage people who did not contribute to the financial gain of the Reich.

**Vater**: Father.

**Volk**: People. During the Nazi era, the term was synonymous with people of Aryan heritage, their ideal Master Race.

**Wehrmacht**: The German armed forces.

**Work camps**: concentration camps.

# Acknowledgements

This book's journey from idea to publication took years. I've been blessed with incredible support and encouragement along the way. I'd like to thank:

Nancy Butts, my instructor at Institute of Children's Literature. She repeatedly urged me to find the heart of my story, and her honest purple pen kept me searching for it;

Elisabeth Angermair, Librarian at the Stadtarchiv München, Munich Germany;

Jeff Bridgers and Amber Paranick, Reference Librarians at the Library of Congress in Washington DC;

David Rose, Archivist at the National Office of the March of Dimes, White Plains, NY;

The amazing members of the Dietrich Endless Mountains Writers critique group, who tolerated a dozen new beginning chapters and endless revisions. Lauren Andreano, Joe Barone, the late Carlton Brown, Phyllis Cohen, Mary Fox, Hildy Morgan, Mary Slaby, Nora Stepanitis, Ann Vitale, Dale Wilsey, Lena Ziegler, and many others. Your suggestions enliven my writing and your friendships enliven my life;

My beta readers – Ann Armezzani, Katie Barnett, Clay Bradley, Joni Bradley, Jalinn Chapman, Phyllis Cohen, Nicole Dixon, Virginia Fiore, Tara Gwyn, Emily Johns, Carolyn Kerkowski, Alyssa Kristeller, Brian Lucas, Abby Mappes, Karin Mappes, Kathy Moran, Michael Moran, Hildy Morgan, Mimi Palmere, Christa Parry, Judy VanHouten, Ann Vitale, Nancy Walter, Anna Wrobel, and Lena Ziegler. Your excitement about this book energized me when I flagged, and your recommendations helped me fine tune it;

My sister-in-law Dana Perrow-Moran and my husband Michael for insightful detailed editorial help;

Uta Dreher and my parents Judith and the late Norbert Grunau for their input about the life and character of the German people;

Jennifer Beemer, for your help with practical matters so I could focus on writing and research;

My sister-in-law Kathleen Moran, for hosting me during the research at the LOC;

Mike Moran, for your encouragement to continue this project and finish what I started. I'm glad you're my son;

Joni Bradley, for listening to endless iterations of plots and characters, reading multiple versions, and reminding me to listen to my heart. You're the best friend a girl could have;

Katie Barnett, my daughter, who accompanied me on the research trip to Munich. I cannot thank you enough for your generous gift of love, time, and support – and for still speaking to me after I got us lost in Munich;

Michael Moran, my husband and partner for life's journey, for picking up the slack while I worked evenings, weekends, and vacations on this book. You knew when to offer help and when to leave me undisturbed to pursue my dream. All my love.

If I've omitted someone, the responsibility is mine alone.

A study guide, a list of discussion questions, and a bibliography of sources used during research for this novel are available on the author's website http://jeannemoran.weebly.com

Contact the author at j44eanne@gmail.com

If you have enjoyed this book, please leave feedback on Amazon or Goodreads. Thank you!